Heartbeat Away

Laura Summers grew up in South London and was a teacher before becoming a scriptwriter for many popular children's TV series.

Her first novel, *Desperate Measures*, won the AMI Literature Award and was nominated for the Carnegie Medal and shortlisted for the Waterstone's Children's Book Prize.

Praise for *Desperate Measures*:

'An exciting adventure with plenty of drama and humour . . . Thought-provoking and moving.'
Books for Keeps

'A fabulous book . . . incredibly poignant.'
Birmingham Post

LAURA SUMMERS

PICCADILLY PRESS • LONDON

First published in Great Britain in 2011
by Piccadilly Press Ltd,
5 Castle Road, London NW1 8PR
www.piccadillypress.co.uk

A catalogue record for this book is available from the British Library

ISBN: 978 1 84812 109 6 (paperback)

1 3 5 7 9 10 8 6 4 2

Printed in the UK by CPI Bookmarque, Croydon, CR0 4TD
Cover design by Simon Davis
Cover illustration by Sarah Kelly

Waiting

Everyone dreams of something incredible happening to them. Something that'll completely change their life, for ever. Take Leah, my best friend: she's desperate to wave goodbye to the estate and live happily ever after on some sun-drenched tropical island, feasting on coconuts and barbecued fish. My stepbrother, Danny, on the other hand, has set his heart on playing for Man United in the Cup Final, scoring the winning goal. And I know at least three tone-deaf wannabes who are going to win some big TV talent competition and instantly become rich and famous.

I'm no different. I've been waiting two years now for the big thing that's going to change my life, but, unlike most people, I don't really like telling anyone what I'm waiting for, in case they get the wrong idea.

You see, I'm waiting for someone to die. Not any old person, you understand; not Mr MacNamara my maths teacher or Shannon Walters or Masher Crombie, or anyone else I know for that matter. This special person will be a complete stranger. They'll never meet me – in fact, they won't even know I exist. And, although I now spend most of my days wondering and imagining who they are and what they're like, I'm never really going to know anything about them – they might as well belong in a parallel universe.

So, as I lie here, too exhausted to move, they'll be going about their life, rushing around doing whatever it is that they do all day, then falling asleep at night, totally unaware that I exist – terrified, but waiting.

Waiting for them to die so that I can live.

1

'Becky . . . Becky . . . come on, love, wake up.'

I slowly open my eyes. Mum's standing over the sofa in her dressing gown. I've been sleeping down here in the sitting room because I can't manage the stairs to my bedroom any more. It's like hiking up Mount Everest in my slippers.

She reaches across to the sideboard with all my cross-country trophies, and switches on the little table lamp. Her face is creased with sleep and her short hair's sticking up all over the place. I glance at the clock on the mantlepiece. Twenty to two.

'What's happened?'

My stepdad, Joe, is in the hall, talking on the phone in low tones.

'Is it Gran?' I ask. 'Is she OK?'

'She's fine. It's the hospital. They want you in right away.'

'Now?'

Mum nods and looks at me warily.

'But it's the middle of the night!'

'They think they might have a new heart for you.'

My clapped-out old one misses a beat. 'But . . .'

'We've got to get going right now. Gran'll be here for Danny.'

Mum's holding a blue backpack. It's the one we bought when I first went on the transplant list. I stare at it blankly. It's so long ago, I no longer have any idea what I carefully packed inside.

'Mum . . .'

'What, sweetheart?'

'I . . . I can't go.'

'What d'you mean?'

'I can't go,' I say more firmly. Mum looks at me anxiously. 'I'm not ready,' I tell her.

'Not ready?' She looks at me aghast. 'Becky, we've waited months for this!'

'It's night-time . . .' I'm clutching at straws now. 'I haven't washed my hair.' I burst into tears. Mum hugs me like I'm four years old, instead of fourteen. Every night for the past few months, I've been having the same nightmare. And each night it's become scarier. I'm being chased by a pack of red-eyed wolves. Totally exhausted, I stagger down to a river, but something's in there, something that churns the water in its excitement to be fed. On the opposite bank, everyone is shouting and yelling at me to get across because it's my only chance, but I never find out if I make it, because every night I wake to the sound of my heart pounding in my ears. I'm drenched in sweat and gasping for air.

'It'll be all right, Becky,' says Mum.

'Are you sure?' I look at her long and hard. She doesn't answer.

'I'm frightened,' I say.

'You'd be silly if you weren't,' she whispers, her voice shaking, as she hugs me tighter and strokes my unwashed hair.

I think about my nightmare and realise I have a choice. I can stay at home, wash my hair and slowly die over the next few months, or I can go to the hospital, let someone cut out my heart, sew a dead person's heart in its place and then, just maybe, make it safely to the other side.

Wherever that may be.

2

Joe drives us through the rain to the hospital. He and Mum start by chatting brightly, but after a while they run out of steam and fall silent, so he puts the radio on. A cheesy pop song blares out about someone giving someone else their heart. Mum glares at him, he catches on and quickly changes stations, tuning into a late night phone-in 'for all those broken-hearted souls out there'.

'Oh, for goodness' sake!' she hisses.

Slumped in the back of the car under a fleecy blanket, I watch a large drop of rain slowly trickle down the window.

'It's all right, Mum,' I whisper breathlessly, 'it doesn't matter,' but she flicks the radio off and we drive on in silence for the rest of the journey. There isn't much traffic and most of the shop-fronts have their metal shutters rolled down. We pass a group of people making their way home after a night out, laughing and joshing each other without a care in the world.

There is a girl, much older than me but with long dark

hair, just like mine used to be before it was all cut off because it's easier to manage. She has her arm round her friend's shoulder and they're dancing along the wet pavement, singing in the rain. I catch her eye as we drive past and she impulsively smiles and waves. I slowly wave back, but instantly feel mean. She has no idea that I'm desperately wishing I could swap places with her, right now.

It's nearly three o'clock when we get to the hospital. Even though it's the middle of the night, the place is bustling with people. Joe goes off to find me a wheelchair, then we check in at the reception before they wheel me up to the Cardiac Unit.

I'm glad Mum is allowed to stay because about an hour later, when the nurse puts the clear plastic mask over my face, I suddenly panic. I'm expecting to smell gas or something, but there's nothing. I have a terrible thought. What if the anaesthetic doesn't work and I'm still awake while they operate?

3

'It's all over now, Becky . . . Wake up, Sleeping Beauty.'

I don't have the faintest idea who's talking to me, or what is all over, but my throat feels sore and my mouth is as dry as a pre-school sandpit.

'Shall I get you some ice to suck?' asks a different, chirpier voice.

I'm not sure about this either, but I nod anyway, then direct all my energy into forcing my eyes open. I immediately wish I hadn't. The sitting room is bright. Much too bright. The TV is on and beeping, but the programme is rubbish – just wavy lines and numbers. And someone has stolen my sofa. Totally confused, I look down and see thin plastic tubes attached to my wrist, arms and goodness knows where else. Some of them are linked to the TV.

'How you feeling, love?'

I'm sure I know that voice. Feeling slightly nauseous, I make a huge effort and slowly turn my head. Mum and Joe are sitting by the side of my bed. Behind them, standing in the doorway to a corridor and staring at me, is a tall boy with dark hair and dark brown eyes.

'What have they done to Danny?' I asked, bewildered.

'He's at school,' says Joe.

'You're in the hospital, remember?' adds Mum, stroking my forehead. 'The nurse said you might feel a bit groggy when you first wake up.'

I stare curiously at the large piece of wadding covering my chest, wondering how something so light could hurt so much. From down the corridor I can hear the sounds of doors banging and clattering, unknown voices, and phones constantly ringing. I take a deep breath, sucking in the smell of disinfectant tinged with boiled fish that hangs in the air. Two and two are slowly starting to make four.

'Dr Sampson said it all went really well. Textbook stuff. Your mum and I had a good long chat with him yesterday,' says Joe. There's black stubble on his chin and dark circles under Mum's eyes.

A young nurse bustles in holding a glass containing ice cubes, followed by a woman with a stethoscope round her neck who smiles, says I'm looking good, then starts to check some of the wires attached to me. The boy's gone. A little girl, hunched in a wheelchair and clutching an enormous furry pink rabbit, is wheeled past the doorway by a porter.

'Yesterday?'

'It's Wednesday afternoon. You've had your new heart for over forty-eight hours,' says Mum happily. 'You're not to worry any more, Becky,' she adds. 'Everything's going to be all right from now on.'

* * *

After Mum and Joe have gone home for the first time in two days and I'm finally alone in my room for a few minutes, I look down at my chest again, covered by the piece of wadding. Inside me, my new heart is beating away, rhythmically and steadily, slowly bringing me back to life. My new life.

At last I am going to be strong and well enough to do all the things I haven't had the energy to even think about over the last two years. Soon I'll be able to go out with my friends, even start cross-country training again. I take a long, deep breath and exhale slowly. I can't wait to feel the freedom of running flat out in the open air and knowing nothing bad is going to happen to me.

A rush of euphoria floods through me, making me tingle with excitement and forget all the pain I'm in. My ordeal is over. Despite all the dangers, I've made it safely across to the other side of the river. I've done it. Well . . . not on my own, I've got Dr Sampson and his team to thank for that. And someone else, of course.

My donor. I don't even know his or her name. All I know is, this person shares the same blood group as me, and a few hours before I received their heart, their life ended. And it suddenly hits me: while my family is over the moon and celebrating right this minute, somewhere else my donor's family is suffering and grieving. As the enormity of this and everything that has happened over the last few days starts to sink in, tears roll down my cheeks and, before I know it, I'm sobbing uncontrollably. The numbers on the monitor race up, higher and higher. It starts beeping angrily, and two nurses rush in.

'I'm fine,' I tell them as they hurriedly check me out, then, visibly relieved, reset the machine. 'Really. I'm fine.'

4

Today, as the effects of the anaesthetic are wearing off, I'm beginning to feel I'm back in the land of the living. The nurses are still checking my temperature, blood pressure, pulse and oxygen levels every two hours, but Dr Sampson arrives and tells me how pleased he is with how it's all going, and a physiotherapist called Sahasra comes to see me.

She explains her name means 'new beginnings', which is very apt because she's planning one for me right here and now, by helping me stand up for the first time since the operation.

I ache all over, despite the painkiller flowing through the drip into my arm so I kick up as much fuss as I can, hoping she'll have pity and leave me in peace.

With a cheerful smile, my protests are totally ignored as Sahasra slowly helps me up. She might as well ask me to go ten rounds with a world champion sumo wrestler.

I've just made it to my feet when, from the corner of my eye, I catch sight of someone else in the room. The last thing

I want is an audience.

'I feel like a performing monkey,' I say, glancing over her shoulder at a dark-haired boy about my age, as Sahasra encourages me to gently walk a few paces on the spot. The boy doesn't take the hint. I don't care how ill he is, I think irritably, I'd never dream of staring at another patient the way he is at me.

Lying back in bed a few minutes later, I feel as if I've just been run over by a train. Several times.

'I'll be back tomorrow and we'll try something a bit more energetic,' Sahasra promises with a smile. 'A little walk, maybe, and a few gentle arm exercises.'

'Lovely,' I reply, looking up and realising my audience has got bored and gone. 'Can't wait.'

'Got to use that wonderful new heart,' she retorts as she walks out of the room.

5

Within a week, all the tubes and drips attached to me are taken out, I'm walking up and down the corridor and they've weaned me from liquids onto proper food again. The meals aren't too bad, so long as they don't give me any meat. I used to love Mum's roast dinners, but now just the thought of eating a ham sandwich makes me feel queasy. Instead, I seem to have developed a passion for peanut butter. I used to hate the stuff.

I have to start taking tons of tablets every day. Dr Sampson tells me the main ones are called immunosuppressants and I'll be on them for the rest of my life, because they stop my body trying to attack or reject my new heart. The big problem, he says, is that they lower the strength of my body's immune system – the thing that protects me against infections – so when I'm back home I'll have to tell Mum if I feel unwell or think I'm running a temperature, because an infection could lead to my new heart failing.

Not surprisingly, I don't want to think about this. I feel safe in the hospital, the ward is cleaned every single day, everyone has to wash their hands and arms up to the elbows with the anti-bacterial soap before they come near me, and visitors are banned if they have a cold.

With each passing day, I'm feeling stronger and more like my old self before I got ill . . . until the morning Dr Sampson breaks the news that I'll be going home later that day.

'You don't look very excited, Becky.' With a mock frown, he turns to the two medical students by his side and shrugs. 'Our patients have such a fantastic time here they never want to leave.'

The students smirk politely as Dr Sampson turns back to me. 'Well, spill the beans, Miss Simmons – what's up?'

'I suppose I'm just a bit nervous,' I mumble, but I know it's more than that. I'm petrified. When I go home, there will be germs everywhere.

'All your test results were excellent. In fact, they couldn't have been better. Your new heart is working beautifully. You're far too well to be stuck in hospital, Becky,' he says. 'You need to be out there, getting your life back on track.'

Mum helps me clear my locker and pack my things, including a huge card signed by my whole form. I didn't want anyone at school to know about my operation, but Masher Crombie lives two doors down from Gran and she and his mum are as thick as thieves, always having a good gossip about something or other. Besides, I know I should feel honoured – there among all the joky comments and get-well messages, Shannon Walters has bothered to scrawl her mark.

After we've thanked all the staff, Joe picks up my bag and

we walk down through the corridors and out of the hospital into the fresh cold air. As I look back one last time, I see someone standing on the grass just outside the entrance. It's the dark-haired boy. Impulsively, I give him a wave, but instantly wish I hadn't as he doesn't bother waving back.

'Who are you waving to?' asks Mum, peering round.

'No one,' I reply.

We make our way back to the car and I'm shocked how everything seems so much brighter, louder and faster than I remember. I've only been in hospital for three weeks, but during that time I haven't been outside at all.

I can't help shivering.

'Cold, Becky?' Joe asks.

'Just a bit,' I reply, pulling up my hood. But I'm not. I don't want to tell him I feel like a prisoner released into the daylight, wondering how I'm going to cope in the big wide world.

We drive past school just as everyone is spilling out of the gates into the street. Mr MacNamara is on duty and he's in full flow, telling Masher off. Shannon's standing behind them, hands on hips, rolling her eyes impatiently and making faces behind Mr MacNamara's back. I spot more of my class among the throng of kids, then see Leah, Alesha and Jodie chatting and giggling as they dive into the newsagent's, to buy crisps, probably. I sink down in the car, not wanting to be seen. I miss my friends, but I'm not ready to rejoin their world yet.

The first thing I do when we get home is wash my hands with anti-bacterial soap. Twice.

6

'Becky! What on earth are you doing up there?'

'Nothing . . .'

'Yes, you are! I can hear all sorts of banging and crashing – sounds like you're herding elephants.'

Mum rushes upstairs and charges into my bedroom, halting abruptly as she clocks the chaos around her. My bed is now by the window, my wardrobe has been shunted a couple of metres along the wall and my chest of drawers stands near the door where my desk used to be. Most of the stuff that was inside the wardrobe is now scattered shamelessly over the floor. I stand on the last little island of carpet and wait for Mum to go ballistic.

'Oh . . . Be-cky!' Mum glares at me disapprovingly.

'I was just changing things around,' I plead, weakly. I glance around the room once more and can't help but see things though her eyes. It looks as if I've been burgled.

'You've been home two weeks! You're not supposed to pull or push anything – let alone shunt furniture around!

What about your scar?' Mum isn't just angry, I can hear panic in her voice. 'What on earth were you thinking?'

I go blank. What was I thinking? I don't really know. Except I've had such a strong feeling ever since I got home that my room isn't how it should be. Things aren't in the right place.

'It's OK, Mum,' I tell her. 'Danny helped me with the heavy stuff.'

Right on cue he pops his head around the door. 'Told you she'd be cross,' he says, holding a football in his arms. 'You coming out, Becky?'

'Maybe later, Squirt. I need to finish my room.'

'Oh. OK.' The smile falls from his face, he turns away and pads off downstairs.

Mum looks at me.

'What?'

'You could play with him sometimes, Becky.'

'He's seven, Mum. I'm not standing around, watching him kick footballs into next door's garden.' I turn away, picking up a pair of shoes from the floor. 'Besides, he's not even my real brother, for goodness' sake.'

Mum gives a small, resigned sigh and turns to go. I bite my lip. It isn't Danny's fault his dad has married my mum.

She hesitates by the door. 'Maybe I'd better just check your scar . . .'

'I'll do it in a minute,' I say. 'Promise.'

'OK,' she says, eyeing me warily. 'Make sure you do. Oh, before I forget, Jodie called. About the school play . . .'

My face falls.

'Come on, Becky, it'll be good for you to go . . . see all your friends again. I told her you'd ring her back, but I'm sure she can wait till you've cleared up this mess,' she adds with a wry smile.

She walks out, leaving me standing among the wreckage that was my beautifully tidy room a couple of hours ago. I look around, confused. I used to love my room so much. Until today, I haven't wanted to change a thing for years. As I turn, I catch my reflection in the long mirror and stare at it, unnerved. Am I so different now I've got someone else's heart inside me?

I examine the pale oval face gazing curiously back at me. My fringe has grown, I notice, but there are still dark shadows under my eyes and my cheeks seem a lot puffier than they used to be. Dr Sampson said the tablets might make that happen. Great, I think, I survive serious heart surgery only to turn into a giant hamster.

I gently pull down my black roll-neck jumper and look at the Frankenstein scar running down my chest. It seems to be healing OK, but it still looks red and angry. I don't like to look at it very often and when I do I sometimes just take a peek at the top. I know it's there and what it means, and that's enough. I briskly pull my jumper back into place and carefully re-roll the material over my throat. I only wear clothes with high necks now.

7

'It'll be really packed – all the tickets are sold, but I've got you a seat right at the front,' Jodie tells me excitedly over the phone. 'You wait till you see Leah . . . or should I say Chicken Number Seven? Trust me, you're gonna *die* laughing!' There's a sudden embarrassed pause. 'Whoops . . . sorry, Becky, I didn't mean that . . . I —'

'Forget it,' I interrupt. 'Look, I'm not sure I'll be able to make it . . .'

'What! Why? You told me the operation went well and you're getting better . . .'

'It did and I am. But . . . um . . . Mum said I mustn't over do things and —'

'Becky! No one's going to haul you up on stage and make you join in! You've only got to sit on your bum and watch, and then clap at the end!'

'I know but —'

'You've got to come, Becks, or Chicken Number Seven'll be heartbroken! You can't let the kid down . . . Pleeeeease!'

There's an awkward silence. I desperately search for another excuse but my mind's blank. All I can think about are the yucky germs and infections I could pick up if I sit in that crowded school hall for several hours. It's winter now and colds and flu are everywhere. People will be coughing and spluttering through the whole performance. Just one cough from some doting parent sitting behind me, and I'll be sprinkled with three million microscopic bugs. I shudder.

'I'll try and come . . . really I will,' I hear myself lying.

'You'd better!' Jodie jokes. 'And you're allowed to stay on for the cast party afterwards. I've okayed it with Miss Devine.'

'Great. Thanks, Jodie,' I blurt out as brightly as I can.

'See you next week, then.'

'Bye.'

I put down the phone and go back up to my room, searching the corners of my mind for some convincing excuse while feeling really annoyed with myself. Last year's *Macbeth* was a hoot. I wasn't well enough to have an acting part, but I helped out with the costumes, sewing bits at home when I felt too ill to go into school. I managed to see the play on the last night, when everyone had lost their stage fright and Miss Devine was no longer semi-hysterical from the trauma of rehearsing Masher as Soldier Number Four.

After the performance was over, we all gathered in one of the classrooms, there was tons of food and music and Miss Devine led everyone except me in a conga around the desks. It was hilarious. Mr Patterson, our head teacher, came in and congratulated us all, saying everything went remarkably well, considering Masher Crombie managed to fall off the stage at least once during every performance.

Maybe I will try and go, I think defiantly. Life hasn't exactly been a bundle of laughs recently and Mum keeps saying it'll do me a power of good to get out.

But then I remember the germs.

In the end, I spend the evening of the play in the sitting room with Gran, playing Scrabble. She wins as usual, but then she always puts down words I've never even heard of. I'm sure she makes most of them up.

When I speak to Jodie, she swears she's not annoyed that I didn't turn up, but she doesn't ring so often now and I haven't spoken to her for a while.

8

'Why don't you go outside for a walk or something?' asks Joe.

'No, thanks.'

I'm curled up on the sofa, supposedly finishing work Mr MacNamara set me centuries ago, but quite happily doodling pictures of swans in the back of my maths book.

Why swans? I haven't a clue. I don't even like them. When I was little, Mum, Dad and I had a picnic by a river and this evil, hissing bird flapped up and grabbed my sandwich in its big orange beak before Dad could shoo it away.

But my swans are different. I'm getting the hang of drawing the sweep of their long elegant necks, I can curve them this way or that and still make them look realistic. Feathers are tricky, but practice makes perfect.

'So how about a little jog round the block, then?' Joe persists, drawing the curtains fully open. 'Bit of exercise?'

'It's really cold today,' I say, shading in the beak of my latest attempt.

'Apart from your check-up every week, you haven't been out since you came back from hospital.'

'Maybe tomorrow,' I tell him. But I know tomorrow never comes. I don't want to go outside – I want to stay right here in the house where I'm safe and not going to catch something horrible.

'Becky, Dr Sampson said you must exercise.'

I bite my tongue. I want to tell him to mind his own business. To keep right out of it, because no matter how much he tries to be, he's not actually my dad . . . and never will be.

'Well, how about doing thirty minutes on the treadmill?' He nods at the machine parked in the corner of the sitting room, a bulky and constant reminder that I need to get fit again.

'All right . . . OK!' I say as I get off the sofa, realising this is the only way I'm going to get him out of the room. 'I'm on to it.'

'It'll do you good, Becky,' he says as he goes out.

I put on my headphones, step onto the treadmill, wipe the handle with an anti-bacterial tissue and start steadily pacing in time to the music. As I'm mulling over why I've got this thing about drawing swans, I'm suddenly aware that, instead of just the brown stripy wallpaper, I can see vivid splashes of colour in front of me. Surprised, I screw up my eyes and blink in confusion. I'm looking at green grass and a blue sunlit sky.

My heart thumps faster. Like a succession of photos flashing before me, I see an old-fashioned bandstand with elegant ironwork pillars, surrounded by deckchairs, their brightly-coloured canvas seats flapping in the breeze. Encircling the deckchairs are neat flowerbeds full of white roses. I can almost smell their perfume. I haven't a clue where this place is, but it all feels familiar and, for one brief moment, I'm overwhelmingly happy.

Within seconds it's all gone. Bewildered, I peer at the dull sitting room wall. Everything is as it should be. The clock is ticking on the mantlepiece, my cross-country trophies are sitting on the sideboard, and I can hear Danny outside, playing in the garden. I take a deep breath, turn off the treadmill and, feeling uneasy, try to persuade myself that I must have been daydreaming.

9

I'm on edge for the next few days, but nothing else happens. I chat to Leah online, but freeze when she invites me to come with her, Alesha and Jodie to see Alesha's boyfriend's band play at the Community Hall. Knowing it'll be crowded, I type in some lame excuse. I hear Mum calling me from downstairs. Secretly relieved, I tell Leah I have to go now.

I'm sitting in the kitchen, biting into a sandwich and Mum's saying something to me about going back to school sometime after Christmas. I'm half listening, feeling bad about lying to Leah and staring into space, when out of the blue, I suddenly see an old house with green wooden shutters.

Surprised and alarmed, I try to focus on something else: the taste of peanut butter in my mouth and Mum clattering about making mugs of tea. I'm totally aware that I'm still sitting here at the table, halfway through my lunch, but it doesn't stop me seeing this house with its dark green front door and shiny gold doorbell, which I know will only give a muffled 'glug' when pressed.

The surrounding garden has neatly edged flower borders, brick-paved paths and a big magnolia bush near the rickety front gate and, although there's no sign of them, there'll be daffodils in the spring, and clumps of bluebells under the magnolia. Wondering how I could possibly be so sure of this, I search my memory, but I'm convinced I've never been to this house in my life. And yet, I know and . . . somehow . . . love it. The faint smile on my face vanishes and the hairs on the back of my neck start to prickle. The image fades, and I can hear Mum asking me if I'm OK. I nod, then swallow my mouthful of sandwich with difficulty.

'I'm fine,' I tell her, 'just daydreaming.'

But my mind's racing in confusion. I don't feel hungry any more. Some odd things have been happening to me since my transplant. I think back to that night and can't stop asking myself, who was my donor?

10

'Well, Becky, you're our star patient this year. So far, your new heart's working like a dream.'

I smile in relief at Dr Sampson. 'That's fantastic. Thank you.'

He gives a small, modest nod. Despite his dubious taste in bow-ties, I have to admit he is pretty amazing.

'We're so grateful to you, Dr Sampson,' says Mum. 'Everything's turning out brilliantly. It's like we've won the lottery!'

'We can't thank you enough,' Joe adds. 'If it hadn't been for you . . . Becky, she . . . well . . . she might not . . .' His voice trails off. Surprised at his concern, I throw him a look, but he avoids my eye.

'We're not out of the woods yet, but things are looking very positive at the moment. We'll carry on with these weekly check-ups and then in a few months, if all's well, we'll reduce them to monthly visits.'

'That'll be good, won't it, Becky? No more trailing up

here each week . . .' The room falls silent and I finally realise Mum is staring at me curiously. 'Becky?'

I'm trying to budge the image of some tall gates that I can see in front of me.

'Um . . . yeah, great . . .' I say, nodding eagerly, trying to look as if I'm not a million miles away.

'Not that we mind coming up here weekly, do we?' Mum adds, not wanting to offend Dr Sampson.

I shake my head automatically, relieved as the gates fade away.

'Seeing our patients less frequently is a sign of our success,' says Dr Sampson with a smile. 'Each milestone you cross is another one we can all celebrate.'

'And Becky is definitely OK to go back to school next term, isn't she?' asks Mum. I knew she was going to ask this. She's been dropping hints to me about getting back to 'normal' for a couple of weeks now.

'Yes. I don't see why not. At the end of January,' replies Dr Sampson. 'You've made a great recovery from your operation, Becky.'

'And it's all right for her to mix with other kids?'

'Becky can't live her life in a bubble . . . although it would be sensible to steer clear of anyone who's obviously ill,' says Dr Sampson, as he turns to me. 'I bet you're looking forward to getting back to school after all this time, aren't you?'

I slap on a grin and nod enthusiastically. I'm dreading it.

'OK. Questions?' Dr Sampson looks over at me.

This is my chance.

'Dr Sampson, I . . . I just wanted to ask about my donor.'

He pulls a face. 'I'm afraid we're not allowed to disclose names, Becky, or any information about them.'

'Nothing at all?' I ask, disappointed.

'The whole procedure is totally anonymous. That's the way it works best,' he says, picking up a folder and peeking inside. 'But . . . I am allowed to tell you that your donor was young, healthy . . . and lived in this part of the country. Donor hearts often have to be flown here from hundreds of miles away. They don't always reach us in such good condition.'

'It really doesn't matter who the person was, Becky,' Mum jumps in. 'I mean, we're incredibly grateful, Dr Sampson, please don't get me wrong, but the thing is, whoever it was is dead now and, although that's dreadful for their family, there's nothing we can do about it . . . except be thankful they signed that donor card.'

Dr Sampson nods then looks at me thoughtfully. 'What do you want to know about your donor, Becky?'

'I'm . . . I'm not sure.' I avoid his eyes and think for a moment. He waits patiently for me to speak. But what can I say? I'll look like a right loony if I start going on about the places I've seen, the swans I can't stop doodling and the way I see and do things differently now.

'It's just . . . well, it's just, since this transplant, things have changed.' I look up at him and he meets my eyes inquisitively, his head on one side. 'I suppose what I'm trying to say is that I've changed and I don't understand why.'

He doesn't answer me straight away. He presses the long elegant fingertips of his two hands together and inspects them thoughtfully for a few seconds.

'Becky, most kids your age will never have to face even a tiny fraction of the difficulties or dilemmas that you've been through over the last two years. Transplant surgery is traumatic . . . even when it's successful.'

'But I feel so different.'

'You're on a cocktail of extremely strong drugs. Some of their side effects are psychological, I'm afraid. You'll get mood changes. You will feel different, but it's perfectly normal in the circumstances. To be frank, I'd be a little concerned if all this didn't affect you.'

'So I might have different likes and dislikes or do stuff I didn't do before the transplant?'

Dr Sampson nods. 'It's possible.'

'But I don't feel I'm just me any more. I've got a part of someone else inside me.'

'It's natural you feel a link to your donor – guilt even. They were a living person and you've got their heart. It's a huge emotional thing. Life-changing. But the organ you've received from them is just purely that – a muscular pump to transport your blood around your body.' Dr Sampson looks at me with his serious blue eyes. 'Would you like to talk to someone about all this? In depth, I mean?'

'Yes . . .' I say. 'No . . .' I shake my head and give a small sigh. 'No . . . I don't think so . . .'

'You'll feel better when you get back to school, Becky,' Mum interrupts, eyeing me anxiously. 'I think she just needs a bit of normal routine, Dr Sampson. Let things settle down a bit.'

Dr Sampson nods. 'We do allow our patients to write to

their donor's families,' he tells me. 'A letter can be passed to them but mustn't have any details of who you are, where you live or any questions about your donor. But don't be upset if you don't hear back,' he adds quietly. 'Some families aren't ready to respond. You've got to remember they've lost someone very precious.'

11

Over the next two weeks, I try to compose a letter to my donor's family. It's difficult to put into words how I feel, and once I've tried to express how grateful I am, I don't know what else to say. What can I say? I'm alive; my donor's dead. Just by writing to his or her family I'm rubbing this cold hard truth in their faces. I'm worried I'll say the wrong thing and upset them more.

After all the odd things that have happened to me recently, I desperately want to know more about my donor, but, even if I knew where to start, I'm not allowed to ask. I'm a stranger writing to other strangers and we have to remain this way for ever. I come to a stumbling halt on my fifth attempt, the day before Christmas Eve.

It's late. I've been going round and round in circles, trying to put the right words in the right order, and in the end I bundle all the letters into the back of the drawer in my desk. I get into bed, deciding I'll try again after Christmas. This time of year is bound to make everything worse for them.

Christmas is about being with your family.

As I shut my eyes, thoughts of Dad flood into my head. I try to picture his face, but it's so long since I've seen him, his features appear blurry and faded like in an old photograph. A lump forms in my throat as I wonder where he's living now and whether he ever even thinks about me. Throughout the night, I dream about him coming home again.

When I wake quite late the following morning, my room is unusually bright. I lift the curtain and peek through the window to discover our street draped in a thick white blanket of snow.

The peacefulness outside is punctuated only by the excited shrieks and yells from neighbouring kids having snowball wars and rolling huge lumpy snowmen in their back gardens.

'Becky, it's been snowing!' yells Danny, banging furiously on my bedroom door as if it's a national emergency. 'There's tons and tons of it!'

'I know, you dingbat!'

He bursts into my room dressed in about six layers of clothing including two hats, one jammed down on top of the other. I suppress a giggle as he rushes over to my window, peering out to check that the view from my room is no different to his. He whoops in delight. 'Whaaaaahay! I'm going to make a giant snowman! Big as this house! Race you out there!'

For a second, I feel a tingle of excitement. Then, as I stare out of my window, I have another vision. I'm inside some sort of van, being driven through an icy, snow-covered street. I'm celebrating. There's joking and laughing until, without warning, we skid out of control and come to an abrupt halt. I'm frightened now. Someone's yelling. Distressed, I finally realise it's Danny.

'Come on, Becky!' he's shouting. 'Why are you just sitting there like a big fat lemon?'

I look up and shudder. My heart's thumping and Danny's jumping up and down in excitement by my window. One of his two hats falls off onto the floor and he scoops it up and jams it back on top of the other as, through the window, I glimpse a small girl with long, dark hair, standing in the road, crying.

And I don't know why, but tears start to prickle in my eyes too. For a brief moment, I want to rush out there and tell her it's all right. Not to cry. Confused, I quickly turn away so Danny doesn't see my face.

'You coming out to play or what?' he asks.

'No,' I mumble, quickly wiping my eyes with the back of my hands..

'You're so boring, Becky! Your head could fall off and you wouldn't even notice!' he shouts, running out of my room and charging down the stairs.

I look back out of the window but the girl's gone. Was she real, I suddenly wonder, or did I imagine her too? Bewildered, I fling open the window and crane my head left and right in case she's further along the street, but there's no sign of her. I tell myself that she must be one of the neighbouring kids from along the road.

Downstairs, Danny runs out of the front door, slamming it noisily behind him. He dances onto the lawn, scoops up huge handfuls of snow and flings them joyfully into the air. I watch him for a minute, deciding that snow is for tough, bounce-proof kids like him to roll around on, get soaked by and catch colds in. I realise I'm shivering, so I lean back inside and close my window, but it doesn't help.

As I try to block out the memory of that girl's tearful expression, I pull on an extra jumper and glance around my room. It still doesn't seem right. I can't relax. Carefully and quietly, so no one will hear, I push my desk back to where it was a few days ago. This looks worse.

Suddenly I know exactly what's wrong. It's been staring me in the face since I got home from hospital, but I haven't twigged. My wallpaper. Huge sugary-pink tea roses splattered onto a pale peachy-pink background. I chose this wallpaper when I was seven and Dad was living with us. I've loved it for years. I still love it. It's a link to him. I bite my lip to stop myself from getting upset, because, despite all this, I realise it just has to go. Right now.

12

I hurry downstairs. I can hear Mum and Joe's voices from the sitting room. A few months ago, I'd over-heard Mum telling Gran that she was dreading Christmas this year because I was getting so weak. She hadn't said a single word to me about how worried she was, but she didn't need to. Day by day she'd become quieter and quieter, while Joe made up for her long brooding silences by forcing himself to be unnaturally jolly. I realise now she'd been wondering if I'd still be alive on Christmas Day.

Now my operation has been successful, it's as if a huge heavy cloud has been lifted. They're both like a couple of over-excited kids at a party.

I peep around the door and see them giggling as they wrestle an oversized Christmas tree into position in the corner of the room. They don't notice me, so I quickly tiptoe back down the hall and yank open the door to the cupboard under the stairs, where Joe stores all the tins of paint.

Urgently, I start rifling through the tins. Although I have

no idea what I'm looking for, I know none of them is quite right. Then I see a big tin at the back, half hidden by a pile of buckets. Banging my knuckle in my hurry, I drag it out, then frantically rub the dust from the front. It's a chalky blue emulsion. Underneath my unease and panic, I feel a strange stab of relief. It's the perfect colour. I reach into the cupboard again, snatch a roller and the paint tray, then bundle everything upstairs to my room like a thief.

Mum is going to kill me when she finds out, I think, but I don't stop. I can't stop even if I want to.

13

'Becky!' calls Mum from the bottom of the stairs.

'I'll be down in a minute!' I call back, wiping a smudge of blue paint from my face as I warily check out my handiwork. It isn't the most professional job in the world, I have to admit, but all my wallpaper is well and truly covered. Unfortunately, so is some of my carpet, and my desk and wardrobe are splattered with several random blobs. Despite the mess, despite how I loved my room as it was, despite not understanding why I've just done what I've done, I feel *so* much better. I can breathe now. My room's the colour of the sky on a clear cloudless day. I shove the paint tray, roller and the empty tin of paint under my bed, and head downstairs to the kitchen.

'Joe's been shopping,' says Mum with a grin, nodding at a load of brown paper carrier bags sitting on the table.

'Great,' I say, forcing a smile.

'Ta da!' he trumpets, whipping out Christmas decorations like a magician pulling rabbits out of a hat. You name it, he's bought it – sparkly baubles, foil lanterns, metres and metres of furry, shiny tinsel, masses of fairy lights, a couple of blow-up reindeer and at least three snowmen.

'And finally!' he announces proudly, producing a huge, tacky Santa doll and flicking the switch on its back.

'Ho ho ho! Merry Christmas one and all!' it croaks repeatedly as its head lolls from side to side and its arms flap manically up and down, like a demented red-coated furball.

'That is sooooo gross!' I tell them. 'It'll freak the pants off Danny!'

'Rubbish!' Mum says firmly. 'He'll love it!'

'It's Christmas, Becky!' Picking up the Santa, Joe starts prancing up and down the kitchen. Laughing and pretending to protest, Mum's swept up in his arms and they dance around the table. As I squirm with embarrassment, Danny rushes in from the garden, half soaked and covered in snow.

'What's going on?' he asks, darting a wary glance at Mum and Joe.

I shrug.

'And what's all that blue stuff on your hands?'

I instantly hide my hands behind my back and try to hush him, but Mum has noticed. She unhitches herself from Joe's arms and looks at me.

'Becky? What have you been up to?'

'Um . . . Nothing. Much.' But it's useless lying. 'I . . . just fancied a change.'

'What sort of change?' Her voice is suspicious now.

There's no point in delaying things. 'I've given my room

a bit of a makeover,' I say uneasily.

Mum throws a look at Joe, then rushes upstairs.

'Becky!' she yells down a few seconds later. 'What on earth's got into you?'

14

Joe sees the funny side, but I can tell Mum is planning on being cross with me for the rest of the day. Although I do feel guilty about painting my room, I just can't explain to her, or even to myself, why I did it. Fortunately, Gran and her sister, Auntie Vi, arrive a couple of hours later, so Mum parks her annoyance to concentrate on welcoming them.

'Ooooh, lovely! Just like Santa's grotto, isn't it?' laughs Gran, as she and Auntie Vi fight their way through all the tinsel.

'Thought we'd push the boat out, now Becky's well again,' says Joe. He takes Gran's overnight bag and gives her a hug.

'Quite right too,' she replies, glancing at me. 'You're looking a picture of health, Becky, isn't she, Vi?'

'A picture,' Auntie Vi echoes.

I manage to avoid kissing them both, in case they have colds. Auntie Vi lives near Gran and has three mangy cats that are always jumping up on her kitchen worktop or are fast asleep on the breadbin. She is carrying a huge, battered cake tin.

'Just a few mince pies, dear,' she says, handing me the tin. Hesitantly, I peek inside. There must be at least forty pies jemmied in there.

'Thanks, Auntie.'

'The other tins are in my shopping trolley.'

I throw a glance at Mum, who fires back a 'You mind your manners' look.

'Auntie Vi,' she says warmly, 'you really shouldn't have gone to all that trouble.' She means it.

'There's nothing quite like a homemade mince pie,' chips in Gran, cheerfully.

Too right, I think, desperately trying not to visualise the cat hairs embedded in the pastry.

Despite Auntie Vi's dodgy pies, this Christmas turns out to be wonderful. The snow outside makes everything inside that bit more cosy, Mum forgives me for painting my room, and her and Joe's good mood quickly spreads to us all.

For the first time in over two years, the house is full of laughter and fun, and Auntie Vi and Gran playing charades is the most hilarious thing I've seen since Masher dressed up as his mum one open evening and managed to fool Mr MacNamara . . . for about ten minutes.

On Christmas Day, as it gets dark outside, we all snuggle on the sofas in the sitting room. Gran is sipping a glass of sweet sherry and reminiscing about the last time she saw her and Auntie Vi's sister Ruby, who lives in America now, while Danny and Auntie Vi battle it out on his new extreme sports

Wii game. Joe pretends he's listening and watching but is really nodding off. Mum leans over to me and whispers, 'Happy Christmas, Becky,' and I realise that I do actually feel OK for the first time in ages.

Going back to school might not be too bad after all, I think. I'm healthy now, getting stronger by the day, and although I've changed a bit since my transplant and a few odd things have been going on, there's nothing I can't handle.

I'm at the top of the stairs on my way to bed when it happens. When *he* happens. Suddenly his face is in front of me. He's staring at me, with fierce dark eyes and his mouth twisted in anger. My heart misses a beat as I realise that it's the boy from the hospital.

I do the only thing I can think of. I scream.

15

'Becky, what's the matter?'

Mum and Joe charge out of the sitting room and crash up the stairs, the panic showing in Mum's eyes.

'Did you fall?'

'I . . . I thought I saw someone,' I tell them, struggling to stop my voice shaking.

'What d'you mean, you saw someone? Who?'

'A face – a boy's face.'

'What boy?' Joe looks puzzled. 'Has Danny been mucking about?'

'Not Danny. This boy was staring at me and then he was gone!'

'Come on, Becky, you're imagining things – there's no one here.' Mum puts her arm around me as Joe checks out the landing and peers into the bedrooms and the bathroom. I bury my face in the warmth of her jumper, trying to block out what I've seen.

'There's no one in here, Becky. It must have been a trick of the light or something,' Joe calls.

'You haven't been knocking back Gran's sherry, have you?' asks Mum suspiciously.

'Course not!' I scan their faces. Biting back the tears, I realise they don't believe me.

'Everything all right?' calls Gran from downstairs. She and Auntie Vi are peering up at us from the foot of the stairs.

A sleepy-eyed Danny pads out of his room. 'What's all the racket?'

'Go back to bed, Danny, there's nothing wrong.'

'Then why are you all shouting?'

'We're not. Becky just thought she saw someone, that's all. But she didn't.'

'Was it a ghost, Becky?' asks Danny, wide-eyed with excitement. 'Did it have its head under its arm?'

My heart starts to pound.

'Don't be silly, Danny, there's no such things as ghosts,' Mum says firmly, as I feel myself breaking out in a cold sweat.

'I want to see the ghost too. It's not fair. It's always Becky.'

'There are no ghosts in this house, Danny. Sorry to disappoint you. Now back to bed.' Joe starts guiding Danny back to his room.

'Spirits of the dead,' I hear Auntie Vi say in a loud whisper. 'Can't make their way over to the other side. Something's stopping them.'

'That's enough, Vi,' says Gran. 'You're frightening the children.'

'No, she's not,' says Danny.

And she isn't. I'm already terrified.

16

I see the boy once again before I go back to school.

I'm busy searching through the bottom of my wardrobe for my French textbook. I'm not sure why, but I turn my head and he's there, standing just inside my bedroom doorway. I gasp as his fierce expression catches me unawares, and my heart thumps louder and harder, not just through fear, but almost as if it recognises him.

I'm petrified, but I have to speak to him. I try to say something, but my mouth's dry and the words won't come out. Another second and he's gone. My blood runs cold. Could this boy be my donor?

Shocked, I try to push away this thought, but it refuses to budge and won't let me ignore it. Auntie Vi's words about 'spirits of the dead' ring in my ears, giving me goosebumps. My head aches as I try to make sense of it all. If my donor's haunting me, I reason desperately, why am I seeing other things too – that park, the house with the shutters and that dark-haired girl?

I head into the bathroom, bend over the sink and slosh cold water onto my face. As I look up, instead of my own reflection in the mirror, I'm staring at a boating lake with a bramble-covered island. Terrified, I try to squint away the image. When I open my eyes again, it's gone, but for a few moments I'm sure I can still hear the persistent slap-slap of water as it laps against the concrete rim of the lake.

By Monday morning, I'm just relieved to be going back to school. The previous night, I laid out my uniform and packed my rucksack – something I've never ever done, even before I was ill. I'm sleeping badly, and I wake early before my alarm goes off. I'm up and ready within half an hour.

'You're keen, Becky,' says Joe as I hurry into the kitchen and start sorting out all my tablets for the day.

'Course she is, Joe,' Mum says. 'Her friends have been back weeks already; she hasn't seen them for ages.'

I let them think this is why I'm so eager. It is partly true; although I've chatted to Leah, Jodie and Alesha online and they've invited me to parties and to go shopping with them, each time the thought of all the germs I might pick up stopped me going. I'm missing them now and I want to catch up on all the gossip first-hand. I'm even curious to see if Masher and Shannon are still an item, or if there's been a ceremonial dumping. But the real reason I want to get back to school is that, just for a while, I'm desperately hoping I'll be able to forget all the weird stuff that's been happening to me over the last few weeks.

17

'Now, you're sure you've got everything?' asks Mum, pulling up to park a short way from the school gates.

'Yeah. Think so.' I glance nervously through the car window at the hordes of kids thronging into the playground, laughing and shouting and chatting to one another. After so many months at home, I've forgotten how crowded and noisy schools are. I'm not sure I can do this, I think, panicking. Then through the sea of white, red and grey, to my relief, I spot Leah and Jodie, scanning the playground, looking out for me.

'Don't forget you can text me if you need to,' Mum's saying as she eyes me warily. 'You will do that, won't you, Becky? Not that I think for one minute there's going to be a problem.' The corner of her mouth twitches up into a smile.

'I'll be fine, Mum, don't worry,' I reply, determined to convince myself as much as her that I will be all right. But, gripping the strap of my school bag, I still hesitate, sitting rooted in the car seat and unwilling to take that first giant step out.

I glance at my watch. Five to nine. It's now or never. I fling open the door.

'Bye, then. Love you,' I say, scrambling out of the car. I brave it through the school gates, hurrying over to Leah and Jodie. A gaggle of Year Seven boys chasing a football storm across my path, so intent on their game they almost knock me over. I step back out of their way, but bump into two older girls gossiping together.

'Watch it!' the tallest one snaps as the other stares frostily at me through her purple mascaraed lashes.

'Sorry,' I mumble.

'Becky!' I hear someone call.

I spin round. It's Alesha.

'Becky! It's really you!' she yells, rushing forward to hug me.

I'm really pleased to see her but I can't stop myself: I draw back.

'What's the matter?'

'Nothing,' I lie. I force myself to hug her, secretly hoping she doesn't have a cold or anything. 'It's so good to be back.'

18

'So I'm sure we're all really glad to welcome Becky back to school after what has been a very long absence.' Miss Devine flashes me one of her most beaming and gummiest smiles. 'I think I can safely say we've all missed you. And I hope you'll soon settle back into a routine, Becky, ready for next year when you start your GCSE courses.'

'Thanks, Miss Devine.' Feeling my cheeks burning, I glance over at Shannon, who's busy filing her nails a couple of desks away, and has obviously missed me as much as a large hole in the head. She leans sideways, sniggers and whispers something to Masher, who's sprawled behind the desk between us.

'Shannon, is there something you'd like to share with us all?' asks Miss Devine brightly.

Don't, I think, groaning silently. Please don't encourage her to 'share' anything with us. I close my eyes in disbelief and wait. Three years teaching the likes of Shannon Walters should surely have taught Miss Devine something.

'I was just wondering how Becky feels getting a new heart and stuff,' she asks sweetly.

The whole class turns and stares at me. I can feel myself sinking down into my chair as Miss Devine jumps in and answers for me.

'I think she's probably very grateful, aren't you, Becky?'

I nod, blushing from the neck up.

'Yeah, I know that, but I mean, you know, now she's got a bit of someone else's body inside her. That's not very nice, is it? I mean they could be anyone.'

'Only someone dead,' chips in Masher.

'That's enough, Jake,' says Miss Devine as Masher and a few of his mates snort with laughter.

'Well, I'm just saying,' continues Shannon, as she casually flicks her long, tousled hair over her shoulder, 'I wouldn't fancy it if it was me.'

'Then I think you're probably very fortunate that it wasn't you, Shannon. Becky was seriously ill before her transplant.' Miss Devine throws me an apologetic smile. 'Right. Let's move on. Get out your exercise books ready to make a few notes, please.'

Miss Devine turns back to the white board and starts writing. After exchanging a sideways smirk with Shannon, Masher leans over to me and whispers, 'Hey, Becky-Mouse, show us your scar!'

I put my head down and start writing the date in my exercise book, pretending to ignore him, but this to Masher is like waving a red rag to a bull.

'Your gran told my mum it was this long!' he announces

loudly so the whole class hears, separating his hands until they're about half a metre apart. Darren and Wesley start sniggering, which encourages Masher to pull his arms even further apart.

'No, sorry. *This* long!' he says, grinning smugly, lapping up the attention from his audience.

'You're so immature, Masher,' says Leah, rolling her eyes at me in sympathy.

Normally I wouldn't rise to Masher's wind-ups, but I still feel upset and annoyed with Shannon and those emotions are turning to pure anger as they bubble up inside me.

'Shut up, Masher,' I hiss furiously. 'You're not funny.'

'Unlike you, freak girl,' Shannon says, with an angelic smile on her face.

Miss Devine turns round from the white board. 'Thank you Shannon, that's quite enough,' she says firmly. 'And you can stop waving your arms about, Jake Crombie. Detention tonight, both of you.'

'Oh . . . what?' chorus Masher and Shannon. 'That's not fair, miss!'

I exchange glances with Leah, who's doing her best to control the smirk on her face, then catch Shannon's eye. If looks could kill, I'd be vaporised on the spot.

19

'Just ignore Shannon and Masher,' Leah is telling me as we hurry through the rain across the wet playground to the dining hall.

'She's a cow and he's a complete twazzock,' Alesha adds dismissively.

'Yeah, and Alesha should know all about Masher,' Jodie says mischievously. 'She went out with him.'

'One rubbish date!' retorts Alesha, pretending to be outraged. 'And probably the worst mistake of my life so far.'

'Was it that bad?' I ask.

Alesha shudders. 'Two hours standing around waiting for him to get onto level ten of some stupid computer game; half an hour climbing through a tiny toilet window, tearing my brand new dress to sneak into the cinema without paying, to see the last five minutes of the most mind-numbingly, unfunny comedy ever made. And the whole evening punctuated by Masher perfecting his fish impression.'

'Fish impression?'

'Don't even go there,' sighs Alesha theatrically.

'He's more immature than my baby brother,' tuts Leah.

The dinner hall is heaving. It's as if the whole school has crammed in and is jostling for space and air. The din is overwhelming. The room smells of rain-soaked hair, hot grease and stale PE kits, but Alesha, Jodie and Leah don't seem to notice as they stride straight through the double doors. I hesitate.

'What's up, Becky?' asks Leah, turning round.

'Nothing.' I shrug, peeking in at the chaos. All those bodies, I think. All those germs.

'Hurry up, Becks, the chips'll all be gone,' says Jodie as she rushes off, making a beeline for the food counter. 'They only do them on Mondays now,' she calls back at me, 'and they always run out.'

'I'm not really that hungry.'

'Don't be daft,' says Leah, taking my arm and whisking me inside the hall. 'It's double maths with MacNamara this afternoon. You've got to have something to keep your strength up.'

I can't tell you what I put on my tray, let alone what I actually eat, if anything. All I can think about is getting straight out of this crowded hall as soon as possible.

Two Year Seven boys approach carrying trays loaded with food, hunting for spare seats. There aren't many, just the odd one dotted here and there. They stop just behind me. Grinning in triumph, the spottier one dives onto the single empty seat beside me, leaving his friend standing.

'You finished?' the lesser-spotted boy mumbles, poking me in the back with a grubby, nail-bitten finger.

As I turn around ready to answer, I see his face suddenly contort. He draws his head back, closes his eyes then, before I can get out of the firing line, he sneezes all over me then drags his sleeve across his face.

I freeze in horror for a split second then leap up, spilling my drink over the table before rushing out of the hall.

'Ta very much,' I hear him call after me as the pair dissolve into laughter.

I hurry down the crowded corridor, shove open the double doors and charge into the playground. It's stopped raining now, but apart from a small bunch of boys chasing a ball around, it's deserted. I make it over to the oak tree, sucking in huge gulps of air. Hurriedly, I pull a fresh anti-bacterial wipe from my pocket and start furiously scouring and scrubbing at my face.

20

'Becky . . . Shall I get someone? One of the teachers maybe?'

I look up to see Leah. My thumping heart is gradually slowing and my breathing is returning to a relatively normal pace. I screw up the wipe into a ball and throw it in a nearby bin.

'No, don't, please. I'll be all right in a moment.'

'What's wrong? Is it your heart?' she asks, unable to hide the concern in her face.

Automatically I reach my hand over my chest and feel the rhythmical pounding through my clothes.

'My heart's fine.'

'Come on, let's go indoors.'

Once inside, we sit down in the empty cloakroom, huddling among the damp coats.

'What's going on, Becky?' she asks solemnly.

Leah's my oldest and closest friend. We met at playschool aged three, when she rescued me from Harry Benson who was rubbing sand in my hair. She chucked her lump of playdough at him and we've been friends ever since. She's one of those girls who knows what to do, whatever happens, probably because she's always looking after her little brother. 'I'm just really worried about getting ill again,' I tell her.

'But I thought you were OK now?'

'I am . . . but it's not that simple. I have to take a whole load of tablets to stop my body rejecting my new heart. But the thing is they suppress my immune system which means I'm more likely to catch colds or other infections . . . which could also make my heart fail.'

'But, Becky, you can't live your life worrying about every little germ. They're everywhere. You'd go completely bonkers!'

I look at her. Maybe it's true: my fears are sending me crazy; that's why I'm seeing things that aren't really there. I bite my lip.

But Leah knows me too well. She knows there is more. 'What is it?' she asks.

'If I tell you, you won't spread it around . . . tell anyone?'

'Course not. Cross my h—' She stops abruptly. We exchange smirks. 'You can trust me, Becky.'

I take a deep breath and exhale slowly as Leah warily scans my face.

'Something has happened to me since the operation.' I begin, relieved to be telling someone at last. 'I . . . I've been seeing things. Things that aren't there.'

'What do you mean, seeing things? What sort of things?'

I shrug. 'It's difficult to explain and I probably am going completely mad so maybe that's why —'

'Becky, what have you seen?'

'Places I've never been to but still recognise. A big park and a street, always the same street, and halfway down it a house with green shutters. And this house, I know every single brick, every roof tile, every plant in its garden but I don't understand, because I've never been there before.' I sneak a peek at her puzzled face. 'And . . . that's not all. I keep seeing someone I've never met before. But it's like I've always known him.'

'Him?'

'A boy. About my own age. Maybe a bit older.'

'So who is he?'

'I don't know. But he's really angry . . . and I think it's my fault.'

'How could it be your fault, Becky? You said you don't even know him.'

There's an awkward pause before I manage to say, 'What if he's my donor . . .'

Leah stares at me. 'Becky, don't!' she snaps.

'Don't what?'

'Don't beat yourself up over getting your new heart.'

'What do you mean?'

'Whoever your donor was, he or she died. That isn't your fault, OK? They signed a donor card because they wanted someone else to have their heart after their death.'

We sit quietly for a moment.

'So am I just going crazy?' I ask her finally.

'Course not, don't be so daft,' she says firmly, but I can't help noticing the uncomfortable look on her face.

21

I miss school the following day as I have my weekly check-up at the hospital. They're running late at the clinic, and the waiting room's packed. After checking in with the nurse, Mum and I sit down on the last two empty chairs in the corner. Sitting next to me is a girl with honey-coloured hair, cut short in a bob. She looks up, then hands me the glossy magazine on her lap.

'Here,' she says, 'it's this month's. Full of incredibly thin models wearing unbelievably expensive clothes.' As she smiles, her green eyes sparkle mischievously. 'Just like last month's actually.'

'Thanks.'

She's wearing a blue, round-necked top, edged with green lace but I can just see the faint, bumpy white line of a scar starting from the bottom of her neck and running downwards. I quickly avert my eyes but it's too late, she's noticed me looking.

'Sorry,' I mumble. 'Didn't mean to stare. My scar's still

quite red,' I add quickly, so she knows I'm not just gawping for the sake of it.

'Don't worry. If it doesn't fade, ask for your money back,' she says with a grin.

I start flicking through the magazine she's given me, secretly wanting to carry on chatting but not quite knowing what to say.

'Want to get a drink from the vending machine?' she asks a few minutes later.

'Yeah, OK.' I glance at Mum who nods. The previous patient, a little boy about six years old, has only just gone in with his parents. They'll be at least twenty minutes, if not more.

We stroll down to the battered old vending machine at the other end of the corridor.

'OK, you need to know this,' says the girl turning to me with a serious expression on her face. 'The coffee tastes like tea and the tea tastes of coffee. Both look like dishwater and both smell of old socks. But, as far as I know, there've been no fatalities from the hot chocolate.'

'Sounds delicious,' I say with a smile.

As we feed our coins into the machine and wait for our drinks the girl tells me her name's Alice, and she's here for her yearly check-up. She's nearly eighteen and had her transplant when she was eight.

'I was born with a broken heart – literally – so when I had my transplant it was the best day of my life. It meant that I finally had a chance of living.'

'So was it all OK?'

'I'm here, aren't I? Drinking this poison?' she says with a laugh. 'Don't remember the operation, obviously, but it must have worked. I'd been really ill before so it took a while to build up my strength, but now the world is my lobster!' She takes a sip of her hot chocolate and grimaces. 'Errr yuck!'

'What do they put in this stuff?' I ask, pulling at the top of my roll-neck jumper, yanking it up so it sits higher on my throat.

'Best not to know,' she replies, glancing at me. She hesitates for a second or two then says, 'I also had a bit of a thing about my scar at first. Didn't want anyone to see it. Then I thought, stuff it! It's a part of me, and what I've been through. Call it my battle scar now. If anyone asks or teases me I tell them I got it wrestling a bear. Actually, it's a great conversation starter with boys.'

I laugh. 'So did you feel different after the transplant?'

'Too right I did! For the first time ever in my whole life, I could play sports, dance, ride a horse – do all the things I'd never been able to do before.' She grins from ear to ear. 'I'm going to train as a riding instructor next year. Can't wait. I could never even have dreamt about doing that before my transplant.' She looks at me inquisitively. 'So how about you?'

'A virus attacked my heart a couple of years ago. They finally put me on the urgent list and I had my transplant last October. But since then . . . I've changed.'

'Who hasn't?' says Alice, nodding then taking a sip of her hot chocolate.

'Alice, after you got your new heart did you . . .' I stop,

unsure whether to continue or not. I take the plunge. 'Did you . . . Do you ever . . . see stuff . . . or have memories of places or people that you don't know and haven't met?'

'Nope,' she replies, 'not at all. Why?'

I start to explain what has been happening to me over the last couple of months since my operation.

'Wow,' she says when I finish. 'I've never heard of that before. And I've met tons of people who've also had transplants. They've never said anything either.'

'I wonder if I'm just imagining it all.'

'Well, having a heart transplant isn't exactly like getting your hair cut. I guess it could mess your mind up big time, if you let it. And all those drugs we have to take can make you feel pretty spaced out sometimes.'

'Becky!' A voice I know well calls from down the corridor. 'Becky! You're next for bloods!'

It's Natalie, one of my favourite nurses. I quickly turn to Alice. 'See you later,' I say before hurrying off down the corridor.

22

We're a long time at the hospital. As usual, I have to have loads of blood taken, together with all the other tests and Sahasra wants to check my fitness level, which means walking and jogging on her treadmill while breathing into a mask, on and off for half an hour. I'm totally worn out by the time I've finished. When we get back to the waiting room, it's empty. There's no sign of Alice. I guess she's had all her tests too and gone home.

Mum and I head back to the car, but from the moment we drive out of the car park, the traffic's terrible. We get stuck in a jam for ten minutes, then find ourselves being diverted from our normal route.

'Oh great!' sighs Mum as we're forced to slowly follow the long queue of cars in front of us down a series of narrow side roads, which seem to be taking us further and further away from the direction we need to go. 'At this rate we'll be lucky if we get home by midnight,' she groans. 'Take my phone, Becky, and give Gran a quick ring. Ask her if she'll please pick up Danny from school.'

I do as she asks and I'm halfway through my conversation with Gran when I glance through the car window. I stop mid-sentence, open-mouthed. There, across the road, are the entrance gates to the park I keep seeing. That same park I've never been to but know like the back of my hand. It's exactly how I've been seeing it, with a wide tarmac path leading up to the bandstand and another path which I know winds its way down to a skateboard area and the boating lake over the far side. Stunned, I stare out of the window in total disbelief.

'Becky . . . Becky, are you still there?' I can hear Gran asking through Mum's mobile as we drive slowly past the park railings. I try to say something but the words won't come out. My palms are sweating.

'Sorry, Gran. Yes . . . everything's OK. But we're going to be late home . . .' I look frantically round for other landmarks – I need to know exactly where we are.

'I'll collect Danny, shall I? From school?' Gran is asking.

Opposite the park, a large old church with a long, dusty stained-glass window squats between two smart office blocks. I strain to read its name on the weather-beaten noticeboard fixed outside. Saint Bar-something.

'Becky? I said, shall I pick Danny up from school?'

'Sorry. Yes please, Gran.'

'See you later, dear, mind how you go.'

I manage to say goodbye then catch a last glimpse of the park before we turn down a side street and it disappears from view.

* * *

When we finally get home, Gran has cooked sausages and mash for Danny.

'There's plenty left, Becky,' she says.

'I still don't eat meat, but thanks anyway, Gran,' I reply, trying not to pull a face as the smell of cooked sausages hits my nostrils.

'I have to cook Becky all veggie stuff now,' Mum adds with a small sigh as she starts to tell Gran about our long detour home.

'That's up near where I was born,' Gran tells us. 'Over the butcher's shop in the High Street.'

As I make myself a peanut butter sandwich, I pluck up courage to ask Gran about the park.

'I know the one,' she says with a nod. 'Opposite St Bartholomew's Church. Your Auntie Vi, Auntie Ruby and I used to go there every week for Sunday school when we were little. And in the summer, if the weather was fine and we'd been good, the vicar let us all carry rugs and cushions over the road to the park and we'd sing our hearts out up near the bandstand. There wasn't one of them newfangled skateboard places though. But we used to rollerskate up and down all the paths and Ruby was always making little boats out of paper to float on the lake.'

'Does it have an island shaped like a horseshoe?'

'It does. With ducks nesting on it, and a couple of herons, if I remember rightly. Great big things they were.' She gives me a confused glance. 'You can't see the lake from the entrance. So have you been there before, then?'

My heart's racing but I manage a shrug and force myself to sound calm. 'Only in my dreams, Gran,' I tell her.

23

Sunday morning. I wake early feeling relieved it's not a school day. After that traumatic first day back, I survived the rest of the week. By Thursday morning Masher and Shannon lost interest in teasing me, and despite discovering I'm behind in every subject, it was good to be with my friends again.

Although I don't see that boy again, he's constantly on my mind. Even now, as I peek reluctantly out of my bedroom window, I can't stop wondering who he is.

It looks chilly outside, but it's sunny with just a few wispy clouds scudding across a bright blue sky. It would be so easy just to get back into my nice warm bed and drift off to sleep again but I know I can't. I've been planning what I'm going to do today ever since we drove past those park gates, and as much as I really want to, there's no way I'm going to bottle out now. I'm determined to pluck up courage from somewhere and see it through.

I pull on my old running tracksuit. I haven't worn it for

over two years now but, being so ill, I've not grown much and it still fits. The elastic around the waistband's tighter than I remember, but it's the closest thing to a psychological suit of armour I can rustle up. The cuffs of the blue top are plenty long enough to stretch over my hands and scrunch reassuringly into my fists; it zips up snugly to my chin and the hood's warm. I push my feet into my old comfy trainers, tie the frayed laces and hurry downstairs, scraping my hair back into a short ponytail to keep it out of my face.

I glance in the hall mirror and do a double take. For a brief moment I almost fool myself. I could be three years younger, getting ready to go out cross-country training. It was just Mum and me in those days, but somehow she never missed a race. Looking closer at my reflection, I feel a faint sense of disappointment. The expression on my face is so wary, so unconfident. The stuffing's been knocked out of me and the old Becky's long gone. I've been changed by something undetectable to the human eye – a microscopic virus – just a few nasty germs which cause nothing but a runny nose and sneezes in most people. I turn away. I don't want to look any more.

'Going for a run, Becky?' asks Joe in surprise as I go into the kitchen. He gave up nagging me to go out jogging long ago.

'Probably just a walk,' I reply as casually as I can, as I help myself to some cereal and lay out all my tablets. 'But maybe . . . quite a long walk. I might be out for a while.'

'Great – it's a lovely day today.'

Danny looks up. 'I'll come with you —'

'No you won't . . .'

'It might be nice if your brother came.'

'No, it would definitely not be nice. You're not coming, Squirt.'

'I was only joking,' Danny mumbles, as he carries on spooning in his cereal. 'I don't really want to come anyway.'

'Well, that's OK then,' I reply, glancing at his head bent so far over his cereal bowl that I can't see his face. 'Maybe we could play a game or something when I get back . . .' I mutter guiltily.

He looks up at me, and beams, which immediately makes me feel one hundred times worse.

After breakfast, I slip into the sitting room, take the old A to Z street map from the shelf and slide it into my rucksack with my purse. I give a nervous shiver. This is the first time I've been out alone since my transplant – Mum's still driving me to school and back.

I nip back into the kitchen and hover in the doorway for a moment, almost wishing Danny was coming with me.

'We can make a den when you come back,' he says.

'OK . . . if you like.'

'See you later then,' says Joe, glancing up from his newspaper. 'Take care.'

24

It's still early and there aren't many people about, just a few dog owners muffled up in warm coats, walking their dogs, or lone joggers pounding the pavements. I walk briskly, purposefully, determined to find some answers. I need to know whether I've been imagining everything that has happened to me recently, or if it's real. And the only way I can find out is by going back to that park.

After walking for an hour, I'm starting to feel tired, so I sit down on a bench by a bus stop and check my map. The streets around me are less familiar now. As I flick through the map pages, I can't believe the park still looks miles away.

A woman with two small children sits down beside me on one side of the bench. The youngest child, a little girl of about two, nestles her sticky face against my shoulder, then shakes her well-chewed bottle in the air, sprinkling droplets of warm milk over my tracksuit. As I try to edge away from her, an elderly man plonks himself down on the other side of me. I'm squashed between them.

I look round uncomfortably. The city's waking up and the street's starting to bustle with people. I suddenly wonder if I'm doing the right thing and I'm seriously thinking about heading back home when a bus draws up. I glance at the sign at the front. It's heading the way I need to go and it looks almost empty. Its doors fling open and I step on.

As it lurches away from the bus stop, I make my way right to the back and dive onto a seat in the far corner, well away from the few other passengers. I take care not to touch any of the rails.

I check the map again then force myself to try and relax, knowing this bus will take me almost to the park. We travel further into the city, but the bus slows as the traffic builds. As we crawl forwards, the driver rests one fist on his cheek. Most of the seats are filled now. I squeeze as far back as I can into mine, taking care not to let my hands, hair or bare neck come into contact with the grubby speckled fabric I'm sitting on.

Suddenly I feel overwhelmingly hot and uncomfortable. I reach into my bag, pull out an anti-bacterial wipe and, using it to protect my fingers, try to yank open the little window above me. It's jammed shut. I take a deep breath, telling myself to be calm, as we draw up near a large museum, and a whole crowd of people surge on, filling the bus as they stand cheek to jowl, breathing each other's air. After a couple of minutes, I can't stand it any longer.

I leap up and make my way through the sea of bodies until I reach the exit doors. I frantically push the bell as other passengers eye me warily. I don't care what people are thinking, I just have to get out of here. As the bus finally comes to a halt, the doors swish open and I leap out into the cold fresh air.

25

I have absolutely no idea where I am. I spin around, trying to get my bearings. The street is crowded with people who stream past me as if I am invisible. Breathing hard and fast, I reel back into a shop doorway, pull out my A to Z and flick through the pages, trying to calm down and make sense of all the lines and marks. Eventually, I find the park on the map, and, fighting away thoughts of running back home, head off in what I hope is the right direction.

Twenty minutes later, I stand in front of a pair of tall iron gates, staring at the view through their bars, with the bells of the church behind me ringing in my ears.

At the end of the tarmac path ahead of me is the bandstand. There are no deckchairs surrounding it now. I summon my courage and step through the park gates, half expecting the path to magically dissolve under my feet. But it remains as firm and bumpy as a tarmac path should on a cold February morning. Even the potholes are in the right places, I notice. The bandstand is littered with takeaway cartons. I step up onto the wooden platform and pace around its circumference. Gently touching the back of a pillar with my hand, I feel a shiver of excitement as my fingers trace over what I already know is there. And I'm right. Scratched into the paint are the words *Mickey Sprucket luvs Shona 4eva*. I wonder who Mickey Sprucket is and hope he still loves Shona.

I step off the bandstand and slowly make my way down the opposite path towards the skateboard area. Across the other side of the park, on the muddy fringes of the boating lake, hordes of ducks, quacking greedily, are hoovering up chunks of stale bread tossed at them by old ladies and small children. On the horseshoe island in the middle of the lake sit five prehistoric-looking herons' nests.

I feel as if I've stepped inside the screen of some surreal film as I walk on through the park, my skin prickling with goosebumps.

Down at the skateboard area, a few lads are practising, their faces set with concentration as they show off their skills to their friends and anyone who happens to glance over as they pass by. Apart from the occasional whoop or yell, the only sounds come from the wheels of their skateboards rattling as they jump and skim and trundle up and down the graffiti-covered ramps.

Immediately, I realise I know the curve and angle of every ramp and slope and also recognise the beaten-up old van selling coffee and snacks parked a few metres away. A faint whiff of frying burgers reaches my nostrils, creeping up my nose and down the back of my throat, making me gag slightly.

Everything is as it should be. And it's as if it's all been waiting patiently for me to re-discover it. Feeling strangely happy and calm, I sit down on a bench, carefully avoiding the end with the broken strut that isn't visible but I know is there, and watch the skateboarders. After a while, the sky starts to cloud over and the sun disappears, making the cold day feel even chillier. I shiver and glance at my watch. I'm shocked at the time. I left home ages ago.

Knowing Mum will be worrying where I am, I guiltily take out my mobile from my pocket to text and let her know I'm OK. Nothing happens when I try to turn it on. I curse myself, realising I forgot to charge the battery last night. Mum'll kill me. She's always going on at me about keeping my phone charged so I can text her from school if I feel ill. 'You never know when you might really need it,' she says, cryptically.

Reluctantly deciding I'd better head back home straight away, I tuck my phone in my rucksack, but suddenly, for no reason, my heart misses a beat then starts to pump faster. Seconds later, it's pounding like a hammer and I don't know why. Frightened I might be ill, I look round, ready to call for help but see someone already coming towards me. I freeze in terror as I realise who it is. Same height, same build, same face, same hair. It's him. The angry boy from my visions.

26

I leap up off the bench but, in my blind panic, drop my bag. I curse under my breath as most of the contents fall out, scattering everywhere. My purse flies open and coins spray and bounce onto the grass. Tablet containers roll down the tarmac path. I scrabble about, clumsily trying to gather everything up, as an arm reaches across mine and picks up my phone.

'I had one just like this once,' says the boy coldly, turning my mobile in his hand as he tries to switch it on. 'Looks like you've killed it.'

'The battery's just flat . . .' I hear myself reply, desperate to disguise the fear in my voice but failing miserably. I keep my head down, only once daring to sneak a quick sideways glance from the corner of my eye. Is this really the boy from my visions? Close up, I'm not so sure. His dark curly hair falls untidily across his forehead, masking his eyes. Impatiently, he brushes it from his face, then stares back at me with coal-black eyes. Remembering that terrifying night when I saw his angry face at the top of our stairs, I wait for the worst, wishing I was a million miles away and trying to calculate whether there's the slightest possibility of out-running him if I make a dash for it.

'My sister dropped mine in my tea,' he says with a shrug. His voice is warm and friendly.

I stare up at him in complete surprise as a slightly lop-sided smile lights up his face, revealing white, even teeth. He holds out the phone and looks me straight in the eye.

'Accidentally . . .' he adds, as he registers what must be the most stupid, dumbstruck expression my face has ever worn. 'Offered to lend me hers. But it's pink, so I gave it a miss.'

I don't move.

'Something wrong?' he asks, obviously unnerved.

I take my mobile and put it in my bag. 'Sorry . . . I . . . I . . . thought I knew you . . . but . . .' I must sound like a loony now, as well as look like one. If Jodie were a fly on a tree, she would be in stitches.

'Yeah, you look familiar too . . .' he says slowly.

I freeze. What does he know about me? He looks thoughtful, then shrugs, puzzled. 'You're at The Academy . . . yeah? It's pretty massive.'

'No . . . don't live round here . . . I just . . .' I trail off.

He stares at me curiously as I snatch up a packet of antiseptic wipes and shove them back in my bag.

'I'd better get home,' I say.

He starts helping me to pick up the rest of my stuff. My head's spinning, I'm completely confused. If this is the same boy I saw in my visions, he can't possibly be my donor. This boy is definitely alive. There's nothing ghostly about him at all. So who is he? Here in the flesh, he's a completely different person. There's no anger. No fierce expression. No threat. His eyes have a faintly sad look to them. But I stay on my guard, I've screamed my way through far too many horror films not to know that the baddie always turns out to be the nice normal looking guy, the guy that no one ever suspects . . .

With everything back in my bag, I get to my feet. Thanks,' I say, summoning up a nervous chirpiness as I back away as speedily as I can. But three steps later I start to feel dizzy.

'You OK?' The boy is at my side, his arm supporting mine, his face all concern.

'Yeah. I'm great. Fine . . . Thank you. Must have got up too quickly. Don't worry . . . I'll —'

'You better sit down for a minute,' he says as he guides me back towards the bench. I do as he says then take a few deep breaths.

'Maybe I should come with you,' he says, picking up and handing me a foil blister-pack of steroid tablets that I've some how missed. 'You don't look very well.'

I tuck the tablets in my bag and glance sideways at him. Can I trust him or not?

'No. It's OK, really,' I tell him. 'I'm fine. Honestly.'

'Yeah. Sure. But I'll be coming with you, just in case.'

27

His name's Sam, he's fifteen and he lives with his family in a flat on the other side of the park. I tell him where I live and he's surprised.

'So why come here if you live miles away?' he asks, looking at me curiously as we sit side by side on the bench.

I shrug and avoid his eye.

'We drove past the other day. Mum and I,' I say finally. 'Thought I'd find out what it was like.'

'Long way to come, though,' he says.

'There's something special about this place.' I reply.

He's completely still, staring down at the lake, watching as a heron swoops low over the water. 'I come here all the time,' he says quietly. 'We used to —' He hesitates, shakes his head slightly, then, forcing a small lopsided smile, begins again. 'They say there's a fish that's been in this lake over fifty years.'

'Fifty?'

'Maybe longer.'

'No way.'

He gives a small shrug. 'I didn't believe it either . . . so last summer we sneaked in after the park was shut. Middle of the night, dead quiet . . . no one around. We threw sweetcorn and a mashed-up dog biscuit onto the water and waited and waited. I was so tired I fell asleep. When I woke up it was cold and my friend looked at me and smiled. He'd seen the fish, all six foot of him, gobbling everything in sight, then slinking back under the surface again.'

'Why didn't he wake you up?' I ask.

'He said the fish would be under there another fifty years, so what was the rush?' replies Sam.

I look at the people in little boats rowing on the lake and wonder if they know about the monster lurking beneath them. I shiver slightly.

Sam turns to me. 'You're cold. Come on.'

As we get up, he looks around slowly, as if he's waiting for someone, but all the skateboarders have long since packed up and gone.

'Sam?'

'Sorry . . . I was just . . .' He picks up my bag. 'Let's go.'

We head back down the tarmac path to the park entrance.

'I'll be OK on my own,' I insist, as we walk through the tall iron gates into the street. 'You don't have to come with me.'

'I know.'

We exchange smiles. And for the first time, the sadness in his eyes melts away and I can't help noticing how good-looking he is.

28

We talk all the way home, but I say nothing about my illness or heart transplant – they aren't the sorts of things I can easily slip into a conversation without killing it completely. Besides, I don't want Sam to know.

When we reach the end of my road, I know that in a couple of minutes he'll turn round, wave goodbye and walk out of my life, probably for good. I'm not ready for that either. Usually the only boys who talk to me are those who want Alesha's mobile number. But, besides being flattered by the attention, there is so much more I need to find out.

I know now that what I've seen in my visions really exists. They can't be a product of my over-active imagination or the side effects of all the strong tablets I have to take. I've met Sam for real and physically walked through that park. I can't be going mad. My visions must mean something. But what?

'I can't work you out, Becky,' Sam says as we walk up my road.

'How come?' I ask, with a nervous laugh.

He shrugs. 'There's something about you.'

I force a smile but don't know what to say.

'I live with my mum, Auntie, three sisters . . . even the dog's female,' he tells me. 'They're all in-your-face bossy, noisy, messy and it's always full-on make-up, boy bands and gossip. To be honest, most days it's a relief to get out. But you're different . . . a mystery. You're so calm and quiet, but underneath . . .'

'Maybe you just don't know me very well.'

'I guess not.'

'That's my house, on the left. With the red front door.'

'Becky?'

I turn to Sam, his dark brown eyes serious and thoughtful.

'Back in the park, why did you say you knew me?'

I shrug, playing for time. Shall I tell him everything? Now's my chance.

I bottle out. 'I . . . don't know – I guess I must have just confused you with some other boy. You know how it is.'

'Course.' He looks disappointed. 'So you often mistake random strangers for people you know, then?'

I force another smile. 'Occasionally.' I sneak a look at his face. He's smiling too. Can I trust him? I desperately want to.

'Or . . . maybe I have already met you,' I venture cautiously.

'How? In a past life or something?' he says with a frown. 'Like reincarnation, you mean?'

'Could it happen?' I ask, searching his face.

He thinks for a moment. 'Knowing my luck I'd come

back as an insect,' he jokes. Then he notices my expression. 'You really believe in all that stuff?' he asks.

'I don't know what I believe any more,' I say.

We stand awkwardly by the front gate. From the corner of my eye I see Danny's bedroom curtain twitch back and a small bored face, topped with spiky hair, press itself against the glass of the window. A few seconds later, Mum opens the front door and stands in the doorway, her face like thunder.

'I'd better go,' I tell Sam.

'Can I see you again?' he asks.

My heart soars. I nod.

'Will your mum kill me if I call for you next Saturday morning?' He glances fleetingly at Mum's furious face.

'Meet me at the end of the road.'

'What time?'

'Eleven . . .'

'Becky!' calls Mum impatiently.

'I really have to go.' I run up the path, watching him as he walks off down the street.

'Becky, where have you been? A walk, you said. A walk! You've been gone five hours!'

'I didn't mean to be that long, Mum. I did try to text you . . . but my battery was flat.'

'We've been frantic! Joe's been out in the car looking for you and I even rang round all the hospitals thinking something terrible had happened.'

'I'm really sorry.'

'Sorry?' Tears start to roll down her cheeks. 'Oh, Becky, how could you?'

29

I don't explain about Sam. I don't really explain anything. How can I? I don't understand myself. If I tell Mum about me seeing things and people, she'll really freak. So I decide to be slightly economical with the truth, and mumble that Sam is just a boy I know. She assumes he's someone from school and I don't put her right.

'You're a bit young to get involved with boys, Becky,' says Joe. 'You've got your GCSEs coming up next year.'

'I'm not "involved" with boys!' I protest, glaring at him, annoyed that he always feels he has to interfere.

'Becky, that's enough!' snaps Mum. 'You've had us both worried sick.'

I look at Mum's anxious face and feel terrible. 'I'm sorry. But Sam's just a friend. Honestly.'

And the weird thing is, although I've only just met him, I feel like I've known him for years. Which is, of course, completely bonkers. I hardly know him at all.

Leah's the only real friend I've known for any length of

time. We've grown up together. We played and argued and made up all the way through primary school; spent long summer holidays dressing up in old net curtains and making perfume out of rose petals. She was the only person I told when Mum and Dad split up.

We stuck together like glue when we moved up to secondary school and swapped homework, gossip and clothes. We were both in the cross-country running team and spurred each other on through races on dank November afternoons. And although she always had to look after her little brother, when I got ill she was the one who texted me to cheer me up on bad days, when just getting out of bed was a challenge.

'Mum,' I say, later that day, when she's calmed down about me being out for so long. 'I don't want you to drive me to school any more. I want to meet my friends and walk with them, like I used to.'

'I don't mind giving you a lift, Becky. It's on my way to work.'

'Mum, please, I'm fourteen!'

She glances at Joe who pulls a face. Suddenly she looks doubtful. I try not to glare at Joe.

'Look what happened today,' she says hesitantly.

'Nothing happened today! I just . . . forgot the time, that's all. I'm sorry I scared you. But you can trust me. Honestly. I'll be all right on my own.'

'I suppose walking will be good exercise,' Mum says finally, 'and if you're meeting your friends, there'll be someone with you. But you must keep your phone charged, Becky.'

'I will. Promise.' I hug her.

It's time to start getting my life back again, I think, as I hurry off to text Leah.

Monday morning, I set off to walk the mile or so to school. Since meeting Sam, I'm feeling braver and stronger. Maybe I've turned a corner, I think happily. Maybe things are going to finally settle down.

Ahead of me, by the parade of shops, I see Jodie and Alesha, waiting for me by the newsagent's, so I call to them and wave.

We head off down the road towards the estate where Leah lives, chatting about her party next month and the nerdy boy Jodie fancies (but swears she really, really doesn't, OK?), and it feels just like old times, before I got sick.

'So, how you doing then?' asks Jodie as we approach the block of flats where Leah lives. I'm just getting ready to tell them about Sam when I see Jodie glance at Alesha, who makes a face back at her and shakes her head slightly as if to say, 'Don't.'

'What?' I ask.

'Nothing,' says Jodie. But they're both staring at me now.

'What's wrong?' I ask, forcing a grin. They exchange looks again. 'What's going on?'

'Well . . . We were just wondering . . .' Alesha begins.

'Leah told me . . .' Jodie can't meet my eye.

My heart sinks. 'What did Leah tell you?' I ask hesitantly.

Jodie flushes bright red and starts biting her bottom lip – she only does this when she's nervous, or Mr MacNamara tells her off.

Alesha threads her arm through mine. 'It's nothing, Becky . . . Leah just told Jodie that since you got your new heart you'd been sort of . . .'

'Sort of what?'

'Well . . . seeing things . . .'

'Really weird stuff,' interrupts Jodie.

'Leah promised me she wouldn't tell anyone,' I blurt out anxiously.

'She only told me,' says Jodie lamely.

'And you told Alesha.'

The pair exchange guilty looks.

'You didn't tell anyone else though, did you?' I ask, dreading the answer.

'No . . .' Jodie still won't look at me. 'Not really.'

My stomach starts to churn. 'Oh Jodie . . . Who?'

'I only sort of mentioned it to . . . Sophie Morgan.'

'*Sophie Morgan*? You told Motormouth Morgan?' I yell at her.

'Yeah . . . but she promised on her sister's life not to breathe a word to anyone . . .'

I'm feeling sick. By now, all our year, if not the whole school, will know that Becky Simmons – that girl who's had the heart transplant – is seeing weird stuff. I spin around as two girls from Year Eight walk past us. One glances at me then whispers to her friend, who eyes me warily.

'I . . . I've got to go,' I mumble.

'Becky?'

'Aren't you coming with us to Leah's?'

'I'll see you at school,' I tell them, and rush off down

the street, feeling their stares burn into the back of my head. Leah is the last person on earth I want to see right now.

30

I walk into my classroom. Twenty-nine pairs of eyes turn to stare at me and the noisy buzz of chatter subsides, leaving nothing but a stony silence. I'm right. Gossip spreads like bushfire at our school and word has already got round. Everyone knows something. The brief Chinese whisper that Leah started has clearly circulated and grown and morphed into goodness knows how many crazy tales.

The crowd of kids standing in the centre of the room quickly parts to let me through, fearful that if I touch one of them by mistake I may contaminate them in some way.

Wesley and a whole bunch of other boys snigger as Darren starts softly humming that creepy tune to *The Twilight Zone*. With her eyes fixed on my reddening face, Shannon mutters something under her breath to Masher, who bursts into a sudden guffaw of laughter.

I want to run straight out of this classroom but I know, if I do, it will immediately confirm all the stupid rumours. With as much courage as I can muster, I finally complete the walk to my desk and sink thankfully onto my chair. As I pretend to be rummaging in my backpack, Jodie and Alesha come into the classroom, followed by Leah who immediately rushes straight over to me.

'Becky, I'm so sorry!' she whispers.

'Sorry for her being a complete weirdo?' interrupts Shannon sarcastically. 'That's a good one!'

'Stay right out of this, Shannon,' Leah snaps. 'This has got nothing to do with you.'

Leah turns back to me but Shannon hasn't finished. She's barely started. 'Excuse me, but actually I would say it's got everything to do with me. And everyone else in this room for that matter.' Shannon pauses theatrically for a second then asks sweetly, 'So hands up who's happy with a complete nutter in our class?'

Darren and Wesley exchange stupid grins then thrust their hands in the air and wave them about maniacally, lapping up the sniggers and giggles from the rest of the class.

'Don't be stupid, Shannon,' Leah protests. 'You're just stirring.'

'Me? You're the one who told Jodie that Becky's gone weird since her transplant. And, if you remember, I said right from the start that I didn't think it was very nice having a part of someone else's body sewn up inside you.'

'Don't listen to her, Becky. And I didn't mean everyone to know. Honestly.' Leah turns to me but I refuse to meet her eyes. This is all her fault, I think angrily. I trusted her and she's completely betrayed me.

Shannon turns to the class and asks loudly, 'So whose

heart have you got, Becky?'

Everyone's eyes turn on me expectantly. I'm cornered. 'I . . . I don't know,' I mutter.

'You don't know? I don't believe it! Haven't you even bothered to ask?'

I really don't want to have this conversation right here, right now, but there's no way out. 'Course I have!' I protest. 'The doctors don't tell you. You're not allowed to know. That's the way it works.'

'And we all know why, don't we? They could give you any old heart. And they're hardly going to go round telling you it happened to belong to someone who was really bad, like a psychopath or murderer or someone. They aren't going to tell you that, are they?'

Shannon's words hit me like a slap around the face. She's right, I think, horrified. My donor could have been a bad person. How would I know?

From the smug look on her face, it's obvious that Shannon's enjoying every minute of this. There's nervous laughter from some of the others. The rest just eye me warily but I know exactly what their looks mean. I'm no longer just plain old Becky Simmons to them. I'm that 'freaky girl with the bad heart' – the one that sees and does weird stuff.

'Your gran told my mum you've gone vegetarian since your transplant,' Masher chimes in, grinning like a monkey. 'Guess what? Hitler was a vegetarian!'

I get up out of my seat and head for the classroom door. I've had enough.

'Becky, stop!' Leah calls after me.

I spin around to face her, the growing anger inside me smothering all other emotion. 'I thought you were my friend!' I snap.

'I am . . .'

'Well, forget it. I don't want anything more to do with you.'

Leah stares back at me, the colour in her cheeks draining away. I look around at the sea of grinning faces, then rush out of the classroom.

31

'Whoooa, steady on now!' A shiny grey polyester suit and bottle-green knitted tie are suddenly blocking my exit. 'Becky? Shouldn't you be in class now? It's nine-fifteen. I think you'll find the bell went at least ten minutes ago, young lady.'

I bite my lip. I might be completely distraught but I still have a small sliver of dignity left in me. There's no way I'm going to start blubbing over MacNamara.

'Are you feeling all right?' he asks, peering at me over the top of his bi-focal glasses.

'Not really, sir,' I mumble, not daring to lift my head and meet his eye. I wonder if the wave of rumours about me has hit the staff yet.

'I suppose you'd better get yourself down to the office then, pronto,' he says finally. 'Mrs Andrews'll sort you out.'

'Yes, sir.'

He hurries away, dismissing me without another thought.

Down in the office, Mrs Andrews is busy, so after a quick check that it isn't anything to do with my heart, she sits me down in the sick room. It's some time now since I've been in this chilly, sunless room, but in the months before my operation it was my second home.

Shortly before breaktime, Mrs Andrews finally susses out that I'm not actually ill, so she sends me back to join my class. There are about ten minutes left before the bell goes so I dive into the girls' loos and lock myself in a cubicle.

Completely unhygienic, and the last place I'd choose to spend my time, it's the only place I can think of where I can get away from everyone. I get a teen mag out of my backpack and spread it over the lid of the toilet seat, careful not to touch anything, then sit down on it. For the next five minutes, I use up the last of my anti-bacterial wipes to thoroughly clean my hands.

I stare miserably around the graffiti-scrawled cubicle and catch sight of the words *BECKI SIMMONS IS A SI CO* scribbled several times in huge letters with a thick black marker pen. I close my eyes and desperately try to visualise myself somewhere else, anywhere but this depressing, smelly toilet cubicle.

Within seconds, I'm looking at a big wire-fenced space. It's floodlit and the night air is chilly. Out of the blackness, I catch glimpses of faces with blurred features. There's a fleeting glance or nod or gesture from people who seem to know me as well as I'm sure I know them.

Escaping into my other world still frightens and disturbs me, and I jump as the breaktime bell rings shrilly and the real world suddenly intrudes. Outside in the corridor, doors bang and loud voices erupt as everyone spills out of the classrooms. I shudder as my vision fades.

32

I begin to spend a lot more time on my own at school. You'd think that this would be pretty difficult in a place where eighteen hundred kids and an army of teachers spend seven hours a day, five days a week, but I soon discover that there's plenty of truth in the saying 'you can be alone in a crowd'.

I sit at a single desk at the back of the classroom in most lessons, eat a packed lunch in the cloakroom on my own instead of braving the dinner hall, and hide in the girls' changing rooms during assembly. I get out of PE by insisting to Miss Baudelaire that I have to be very careful not to overdo it with my new heart. Petrified she'll be responsible for giving me a heart attack if I so much as pick up a netball, she sends me straight to the library, where I sit out of sight behind the shelves.

But I'm fine. Really, I am. The less contact I have with anyone at school, the better. Not only will I be unable to hear all the stories people are making up about me, I'll also keep away from all the germs they're carrying.

Anyway, to be honest, I don't have to worry too much about avoiding other people, because most of them give me a wide berth anyway. People I used to be friendly with look away or change direction when they see me coming. Of course, Masher and Shannon keep up a constant barrage of teasing but luckily, apart from registration, we're only together in a few other lessons. I soon learn to avoid the places where I know they hang out, and if I see either of them heading my way I try to disappear before they see me. I'm still walking to school, but I don't see Leah, Alesha and Jodie any more. I guess they take a different route now.

I'm still seeing the park, the house with shutters, and lots of other places too. Sometimes I see a tall blond-haired girl and other people that I can't put names to. So, although I have no control over what I see, at least I have company. For better or worse, I'm not alone.

33

'See you later, then!'

'Mind how you go, Becky, and say hello to Leah's dad for me,' Mum calls from the kitchen. 'Ask how his new job's going.'

'I will.'

These two short words fly out of my mouth so easily, but leave behind a nasty aftertaste. But it's too late now. I pick up my bag and gently close the front door behind me.

Sam's waiting for me at the end of my road. I take a deep breath and slap on a smile in the hope it will dispel my guilty conscience. After a truly horrible week at school, the thought of seeing him has been the only thing that's been keeping me going.

'Hey, Becky!'

'Hi, Sam.'

'They let you out then?' he asks with a smile.

I nod hesitantly.

'So what do you want to do?' he asks.

'Shall we go back to the park?' I hear myself say, feeling unnerved as if something or someone is pulling me there.

'My favourite place,' Sam replies cheerfully, peering down the main road. 'We can probably get a bus from here . . . or a tube or something.'

'No, let's walk,' I tell him, secretly shaking off a small shiver. Getting on a bus again, or, worse still, a crowded tube train, would be my worst nightmare.

It feels good to be walking with Sam and for the first time in a week I start to relax and even catch myself laughing once or twice.

'You hungry?' he asks when we finally reach the park. It's already long past midday and breakfast is just a faint memory.

'Starving.'

From the snack van, we buy a giant-sized bag of chips between us, and a couple of fizzy drinks. I pick up the tomato-shaped sauce bottle and I'm about to squirt it all over our chips but suddenly stop.

'Whoops. Sorry. Forgot you really hate ketchup —' I say, quickly putting the bottle down.

Sam stares at me in surprise. 'How d'you know that?' he asks.

I give a nervous giggle, but inside I'm panicking. How *do* I know? I think desperately.

'Um . . . I . . . I don't but . . . well obviously . . . you look like the sort of boy who can't stand the stuff,' I bluff.

'You're right,' he says with a smile and a brief, wary glance at me. 'So, Little Miss Psychic, what else do you know about me?'

I shrug, faking a laugh, as I pick up a chip and pop it in my mouth. Everyone at school already thinks I'm a nutcase. There's no way I'm going to let Sam come to the same conclusion. 'Not a lot,' I say as casually as I can. 'I'm about as psychic as an old potato.'

We walk up to the old bandstand, sit down together on its painted wooden steps and finish our chip picnic looking down at the boating lake, our faces bathed in the warm, clear spring sunshine.

I pick up the last chip. 'How about we save this to tempt that old monster up from the depths?'

I turn to Sam but see he's lost in thought.

'Sam?'

As he smiles back at me, I see the sadness in his eyes.

'What's wrong?' I ask.

'Nothing.' He shrugs.

'D'you want to go?'

'No.'

'What's the matter?'

'I was just thinking about someone I knew.' He pulls a face, sweeps his hand through his hair, brushing it roughly out of his eyes then gives a small sigh.

'Who?'

'You won't know him.'

I feel the hairs on the back of my neck stand up as a cold sensation floods through my body. 'Tell me. Please.'

He's silent for a few seconds. 'My friend, Callum, died about six months ago,' he says quietly. 'We were best mates.'

'I'm so sorry.'

'Yeah. Me too. He was the one that came with me to find that fish.' He pauses and bites his lip. 'Sometimes . . . most of the time . . . I feel I'm going to find Callum here, waiting for me, like he's just been away for a while, or something.'

I put my hand gently on his shoulder, not knowing what to say.

'He was only fifteen,' he adds fiercely. 'People shouldn't die when they're that age. There should be a law against it.' His face takes on the same angry look I saw in my vision of him.

And then it strikes me, like a bolt from the blue. Suddenly I know for sure that I am only alive because Sam's best friend is dead. Beating away inside my body is Callum's heart.

34

A chill spreads through me as I realise the visions I'm having are Callum's memories. Shocked by this idea, I frantically remind myself I've got his heart beating inside me, not his brain. I don't need to be an A* student in biology to know that the brain is where memories are processed and stored, not the heart.

Yet it finally makes some kind of sense. I saw Callum's best friend and this park, long before meeting him here for real.

I realise that all the other places and people I've seen must have something to do with Callum too. I think about how I've stopped eating meat and felt I had to paint my room. Where did that come from? Callum too?

Fearfully, I start to wonder how else Callum's heart might be affecting me. Am I changing? Becoming someone different? Shannon's taunt about me having a bad heart is still ringing in my ears, filling me with dreadful thoughts. I quickly try to shake off my alarm. Callum was Sam's best friend so he must have been a good person. Mustn't he?

I can't stop thinking about Callum as we walk home. What was he really like? My head is pounding with a ton of conflicting thoughts and fears. There's so much I desperately want to find out about him, but I'm scared of upsetting Sam more by bombarding him with questions.

We reach the end of my road and say goodbye. We arrange to meet again and, as I hurry off, Sam calls after me that he'll text me. As I rush into our garden, I check my watch and give a sigh of relief. I'm five minutes early.

'So how's Rick's new job?' Mum asks, looking up from her magazine as I let myself in through the kitchen door. I stare at her blankly.

'Rick . . . Leah's dad? How's he getting on?'

'Oh, um . . . fine,' I mumble.

'Is that all he said?' asks Mum, puzzled.

'Sort of.'

'I guess Leah's having to take her little brother over to her Auntie's a lot more often now.'

'Mmmm.'

Mum shakes her head. 'All that way on the tube.' She gives a little sigh. 'Can't be easy for any of them.'

I force a smile then quickly mutter some excuse about finishing off some homework to get away.

'Homework? Goodness . . . You'll have to spend the day round Leah's more often,' Mum jokes as I rush off upstairs.

Up in my room, as I lift my black polo-neck jumper over my head to change into a T-shirt, I catch sight of the long red scar down my chest. As it heals, it's becoming maddeningly itchy and I have to resist the urge to scratch at it. The weather's getting warmer. Spring's coming. I can't wear these high-necked clothes in the summer, I think, but I hate the idea of anyone seeing my scar.

All the time, I'm worrying whether or not I should tell Sam about my transplant. It's obvious that he hasn't got over Callum's death. How on earth will he react if I tell him I have his best friend's heart beating away in my body? I close my eyes and try not to think about it.

I go out of my room onto the landing and turn on the computer. Remembering that Alice said she's never heard about anything similar to my experiences, I nervously check out a couple of websites to do with transplants, but find nothing.

I bring up my page, secretly hoping Leah is online or has sent me a message. Although she's really upset me, we've been friends for so many years and I do miss her. I'm stunned to see that loads of people have deleted themselves as friends. Wounded, I grimly tell myself that I should have realised this would happen and I need to be tougher.

I have just one message. It reads, *Hey check this out.* Impulsively, I click on it, to see a link that says, *Becki Scar-Chest isn't rite in the head.*

35

For about two minutes, I'm too shocked to do anything apart from stare at the screen in disbelief. Gradually, those few short words sink in.

Instinct is telling me that I'm making a huge mistake and I shouldn't look any more. But it's as if I'm hypnotised by the screen. As I click on the link, my stomach starts to churn. There are so many comments. Most of the nastier ones have been posted by the same person . . . Shannon.

Half a page down and still reading, I hear a noise behind me. Alarmed, I spin round. It's Danny.

'Want to play my new computer game with me?' he asks.

'Go away, Danny.'

'It's really good – it's got giraffes —'

'No . . . go away!' I explode.

His little face crumples and I suddenly feel mean. None of this is his fault. 'Sorry, Danny,' I mumble.

'What's wrong?' he asks.

'Nothing. I'm fine.'

I wonder if I should tell Mum or someone, but instantly reject the idea. Instead, I close the page and frantically log off.

'There,' I tell Danny a minute later as I get up and offer him my chair. 'It's all yours.'

36

Thankfully, I have my weekly check-up today so I don't have to go anywhere near school. I'm dreading going back now. My visits to the hospital are such a routine that I no longer flinch when they say they're going to take a vat of blood or do a biopsy, which means they take the tiniest piece of my heart out through a microscopic tube to test it. It sounds gross but it doesn't hurt and it's the best way of testing whether your new heart is being rejected by your body.

Maybe it's because I've had these procedures done so many times that they don't bother me any more. Or maybe it's because they help to take my mind off what's happening at school. Unlike there, everyone here at the hospital is pleased to see me, and to my surprise I even see Alice again.

'What are you doing here?' I ask, when I bump into her in the corridor.

'Oh, they love me so much, a once a year appointment wasn't enough,' she jokes.

'So is everything OK?'

'Course. Except I'm really annoyed – I'm missing my riding lesson.'

'So why —'

'They messed up my test results,' she says with a groan. 'They've said it's probably just a blip but they want to re-run them all.'

'Oh, bad luck.'

'Don't worry. I'm out of here in an hour, tops, then straight down the stables. So how's you?'

I force a smile. 'Great,' I lie.

She's not convinced. 'Really?' she asks.

I shrug, not wanting to unload all my troubles on her, as Lyn, one of the nurses, appears at the end of the corridor.

'Alice – I thought you had places to go and horses to see?' she calls.

'I'm coming! I'm coming! Get your sharpest needle ready.' She turns to me and smiles. 'Sorry, got to go.' Her green eyes look serious for a moment. 'Here's my mobile number,' she says, scribbling it on a scrap of paper then handing it to me. 'Text me or ring if you want to talk.'

'Thanks,' I tell her. 'I will.'

'And come riding with me one day . . . we'll have a great time!' she calls as she follows Lyn through the double doors.

I make my way back to Dr Sampson's consulting room. Mum's there with him, waiting. Everything is fine. So much so, Dr Sampson says we can change to monthly checks. I expected Mum to be over the moon, but for some reason she's unusually quiet the whole way home. Something's bothering her.

'Joe spoke to Rick last night,' she says finally, as she opens our front door. 'He didn't get that job.'

I feel my face reddening. Joe comes out of the kitchen and stands in the hall, looking at me with a disappointed expression. I can't help feeling angry that Mum has waited until he's around before she tells me off.

'You weren't round at Leah's yesterday, were you?' she continues.

'Becky,' says Joe sternly, 'why did you lie to us?'

'I . . . I don't know —'

'Where were you?'

I glare at Joe, suddenly filling with anger. 'It's none of your business!' I shout at him. 'You're not my dad! I don't have to tell you anything!'

'Becky,' says Mum quietly, 'we want to know where you were.'

'Nowhere . . . I was just out. I'm fourteen! Do you always have to know exactly where I am?'

'Yes. You've been very ill, Becky.'

'But I'm fine now, aren't I? Dr Sampson has just said he doesn't want to see me again for another whole month. He wouldn't say that if he didn't think I was well.'

'Becky, you're not like other girls your age —' says Joe.

'I am!' I protest furiously. 'Don't you dare say things like that! And I don't need to be fussed over all the time like I'm going to break any minute!' I shout, running upstairs.

'Becky!' calls Mum after me.

'Leave her,' I hear Joe say.

I dash into my room, throw myself on my bed and sob like a five year old.

I stay in my room all evening. Mum comes in at about ten and sits down on the edge of my bed. She doesn't say anything but strokes my hair for a few seconds.

'I'm sorry, Mum,' I whisper.

She puts her arms round me and hugs me tight. 'It's not that we don't want you to go out, Becky,' she says. 'I know it's not good for you to be wrapped in cotton-wool.'

'I wasn't on my own,' I tell her. 'We just spent the day at the park.'

'We?'

'Sam and me.'

'Sam.' She thinks for a second or two then nods. 'That boy who was here the other day?'

'He's a really nice lad, Mum. You can meet him. You'd like him.'

'I'm sure I would,' she says with a small smile. 'I just wish you'd try to like Joe.'

I hug her tightly, but don't reply.

37

Seven a.m. My alarm clock rings. Outside, it's pouring with rain, and I'm so tempted to tuck down deeper under my duvet and not emerge the whole day, but I know this will only delay things, not sort them. I'm dreading facing Shannon and everyone else at school, but know that I don't have a choice. Mum won't let me skip school without a good reason, and I'm not going to lie to her that I'm ill. I can't let Shannon get to me. I've got to be strong, I tell myself. I take a deep breath, then I haul myself out of bed.

Downstairs in the kitchen, I make toast, but I'm too on edge to eat it. Danny wolfs it down as I make my packed lunch, checking the clock every couple of minutes, anxiously wishing I could prolong the moment until I have to leave. Joe pops his head round the door.

'I'm off now,' he says awkwardly. 'Have a good day.'

'Thanks.' I mumble, lowering my head and avoiding his eye.

I know that walking into my registration form is going to

be the hardest part of the day, so when I get to school I hurry through the puddle-strewn playground and slip inside early, before the bell rings. I'm already seated in my usual place at the very back as the rest of the class file in. I lift up my desk, stash away my lunch bag then take out a notebook and start furiously doodling in it, desperately trying to take my mind off the looks I can feel burning into me. Somehow, just drawing the long curving neck and body of a swan calms me a little. I've drawn them so often, I'm getting really good at them now. I start to think about Callum again and wonder what all these swans have got to do with him.

With my head firmly down, I sit on the edge of my seat, ready and waiting for Shannon to start. But nothing happens. Puzzled, I pluck up courage and cast a furtive glance around the room, slowly realising Shannon's nowhere to be seen. Everyone else has arrived. Masher's standing on a desk re-enacting level five of *Death Tomb Aliens 4* to Wesley and Darren, and Leah, Alesha and Jodie sit in a huddle, chatting excitedly about Leah's party in a few weeks' time. The bell rings for the second time. Mr MacNamara bustles in and dumps his old tatty leather briefcase on his desk.

'Settle down now,' he calls amiably. 'Crombie, you've got precisely three seconds to get yourself off that desk and onto your chair . . .'

Masher gives a blood-curdling *Death Tomb Alien* roar and theatrically launches himself off the desk onto the floor as McNamara pointedly ignores him.

Slowly, everyone settles into their seats and the business

of registration begins. I breathe a deep sigh of relief as Shannon is marked down as absent. It's stopped raining outside and shafts of sunlight are falling through the windows and brightening the whole room. I can't help but smile. There is a God after all.

38

Fifteen minutes pass and MacNamara is just dismissing us for the first lesson, when Shannon slopes in.

'You're late, Miss Walters!' announces Mr MacNamara.

She ignores him but throws me a hostile look and my heart sinks like a stone. I don't hang around, but hurry off to PE knowing that at least I can look forward to spending the next hour and a bit on my own in the library.

Or so I think. Miss Baudelaire is off sick. A Miss Strout is waiting for us in the changing rooms.

'Miss Baudelaire usually sends me to work in the library,' I inform her politely.

'Note?' she snaps, barely looking at me.

'Um, I . . . I don't have one.'

'No note – no skiving.'

There are suppressed giggles from a couple of the other girls. Out of the corner of my eye, I see Shannon slink into the changing room, chuck someone else's stuff off the slatted bench, then hang up her bag over the radiator.

'Hurry up and get changed,' Miss Strout orders, then, turning to the class, silences everyone with a single penetrating glare. 'Anyone late on the pitch will make up the time after school.'

I have no choice. I take my kit out of my locker then go over to the deepest, darkest corner of the changing room, as far away from Shannon as possible. I turn away so that no one will see my scar as I take off my school shirt. As quickly as I can, I pull on the pristine Aertex PE blouse and do the buttons right up to the very top. I change into the skimpy wrap-around skirt and pull on my trainers.

Miss Strout starts handing out red and blue bibs. 'You can play midfield,' she announces, dropping a red one onto my lap.

'Sorry?' I ask, trying to work out where on the netball court she means. 'Is that wing attack or defence?'

More sniggers from the girls near me. Miss Strout glares at me, her face like half-set concrete.

'Neither,' she chastises. 'We're playing hockey.' Disgusted by my total ignorance, she throws me a withering look, then continues handing out the bibs.

For the last couple of weeks, while everyone else has been learning hockey, I've been in the library. Apart from knowing the game involves a curved stick and a ball, it's a total mystery to me.

It's spitting with rain outside and everyone's hanging around in the draughty changing room until the last possible moment. Even the sporty girls seem reluctant to head outside. Leah hangs back with Jodie and avoids looking in my direction.

'Get a move on!' calls Miss Strout, marching through the changing room door. 'We haven't got all day!'

Reluctantly, girls start to follow her, each collecting a hockey stick and a pair of shin pads from the pile near the door. I notice most of them have also put mouth guards in. I rub my tongue protectively over my front teeth, trying not to think about how I'd look without them.

'Out the way, Scar-Chest,' mutters Shannon, pulling on a blue bib as she barges past me.

'Don't call me that,' I say. The words fly out of my mouth before I can stop them. I stand rooted to the spot, trying to disguise the fear on my face.

She stops abruptly in the doorway, turning to look me up and down through her mascaraed lashes.

'Why not?' she asks with a smile.

Deep inside me a tiny flicker of anger suddenly ignites and it's this small spark that makes me snap back, 'Because my name's Becky. And that's Becky with a y. Not an i.'

A brief look of surprise floods across Shannon's face, but within a split second it vanishes, leaving her usual smug expression. 'Whatever . . . Scar-Chest . . .' She slowly turns and picks up a hockey stick and shin pads then, strolling outside, catches up with Sophie Morgan. Leah glances warily at me but when I meet her eye she quickly looks away.

Still quietly seething, I follow everyone out onto the pitch. Miss Strout immediately directs me to Shannon's side. To our mutual disgust, we're pitched against one another. As I look down at the hockey stick I'm clumsily carrying, wondering how exactly the thing works, my heart begins to pound excitedly and, without thinking, I adjust my grip so naturally that the stick feels like it's been moulded to my fingers.

Miss Strout blows her whistle, the game starts and I instinctively know exactly what to do. It's as if I've been playing hockey every week for the last five years of my life. I skilfully dribble the ball before whacking it to a red-bibbed team mate. A stunned Miss Strout eyes me curiously, trying to make out why someone who's so obviously in her element tried to skive off the lesson in the first place.

'Mark up, girl!' she snaps at Shannon, who glares across the pitch at me and takes every opportunity to try to whack her stick across my legs when Miss Strout isn't looking.

To avoid her, I head for the shooting circle, as Leah and another red-bibbed attacker exchange passes, quickly gaining ground towards me.

Suddenly, Sophie Morgan charges up, barging in front of me. 'Leah! To me!' she calls assertively, holding her stick poised, ready for the ball.

Leah hesitates, looking from Sophie to me, but then suddenly taps me the ball. Surprised, I stop it, dribble it past the last two blue bibs into the 'D', then take aim, and drag-flick it straight into the net, where it hits the backboard with a loud and very satisfying clunk. A small cheer goes up from the red bibs. Shannon's giving me the evils now as Leah passes me on her way back down the pitch. This time, she doesn't look away but meets my eye with the faintest of smiles.

'Great goal,' she says quietly.

'Thanks,' I reply. My elation soars sky high until it suddenly hits me that I'm no natural-born hockey star, and my goal is no lucky fluke, either. I'm hot from running, but an icy shiver tingles through me as I realise my newfound skill has nothing to do with me, and everything to do with Callum.

39

Conflicting thoughts of Callum prey on my mind as I struggle to make sense of what happened this morning on the hockey pitch. I can't concentrate in lessons and I'm told off for daydreaming. Twice. When the bell finally goes for lunch I hurry back to my form room. Sophie and Shannon are there, deep in conversation, with their backs to the door. I decide I'm not going to hang around, so I slope in as quietly as I can, lift the lid of my desk and grab my lunch bag. In my haste, the lid slips from my fingers and crashes down with a bang. Sophie and Shannon immediately turn around and glare at me, daggers drawn. But then Sophie's expression changes as she smiles knowingly at Shannon.

'Enjoy your lunch,' she says.

I don't hang around to hear any more but head straight out into the playground. I sit down on the furthest bench under the oak tree, take out my anti-bacterial wipes, carefully clean my hands, then open up my bag and reach inside. But instead of my usual peanut butter sandwich, my fingers touch something else. Something warm, squidgy . . . and alive. I scream and reel backwards, throwing the bag onto the grass. I stare in horror at my hand, coated with filthy, germ-ridden soil.

A small brown lump emerges from my lunch bag. Slowly, the thing moves towards the bench.

It's a bumpy-skinned, dirty, slimy toad. And it's been in *my* bag. I shudder helplessly as my stomach turns a somersault and I have the overwhelming urge to be sick. As I fight down the sour acid taste rising in my throat, I realise I know exactly who's done this.

This time Shannon Walters has gone one step too far. She's pushed me over the edge and she isn't going to get away with it.

40

Furiously, I march back inside, down the corridor towards my form room.

'Ignore her,' I try to tell myself. 'Don't let her see how upset you are.'

But I can't stop. I'm beyond upset. I'm livid. The teasing is upsetting, the online comments are nasty, but this is far, far worse and she knows it. I'm going to have it out with Shannon Walters once and for all.

I push open our form room door and see her sitting with Sophie, behind Leah and Jodie.

I stride straight up to her. 'I suppose you think this is funny?' I yell, flinging my lunch bag at her. It drops to the floor by her feet. A dirt-filled sandwich falls out and she eyes it curiously.

'Well, it's not, d'you understand? It's not funny at all!'

'What's got into you, Scar-Chest?' she says, leaning back on her chair and looking up at me.

'I told you not to call me that!'

She looks me squarely in the face and smirks. 'Oh, so sorry . . . Scar-Chest,' she murmurs sweetly.

'Shannon, stop it!' shouts Leah.

But it's too late.

This is the moment I flip. The second I completely lose it. That small spark of anger I felt earlier ignites into flames. They burn so furiously around me that I no longer know or care what I am doing. Gathering all my strength, I push Shannon so hard, her chair flips backwards and she falls with a noisy crack onto the polished wooden floor.

For a second, she doesn't move. She just stares up at me in complete shock. I take a step backwards, staring down at her as Leah's voice echoes in my ears.

'Oh, Becky, what have you done?'

Shannon gives a small tight groan but makes no attempt to get up. Leah rushes forward to help her up but, as she touches her hand, Shannon screams in pain. Darren pokes his head round the door.

'What's going on?' he asks.

'Shannon's hurt,' I hear Leah call to him. 'Go and get help.'

Darren disappears off as Wesley saunters into the room. He looks down at Shannon lying helpless on the floor.

'Oh gross, man . . .' he mutters. Covering his mouth with his sleeve, his eyes fix on Shannon's left arm, which lies unnaturally bent, with the bone poking through her skin.

41

The door of Mr Patterson's office opens and Mrs Andrews emerges.

'You can go in now,' she says in a hushed tone, holding the heavy wooden door open for me. I have only been in the Head's office once before, in Year Seven, when I won a big cross-county race in record time and was congratulated by Mr Patterson before he announced my triumph to the whole school the following day in assembly.

Mr Patterson sits behind his huge desk, writing something on a sheet of paper in front of him. Perched uncomfortably on the edge of a nearby chair is Mum. Her face is pinched and pale and she's frowning. I know that inwardly she's fuming. She barely glances at me as I walk in, stand on the thick patterned rug in front of the desk and wait. Finally Mr Patterson looks up, his expression serious.

'Well, Becky?'

I shuffle from foot to foot and glance sideways at Mum, who's staring straight ahead.

'What exactly have you got to say for yourself?' he demands sternly.

I look down at the floor, totally ashamed. I've never deliberately hurt anyone before in my life. 'I'm really sorry, sir. I don't know what happened. I just lost my temper.'

'That much I already know. Shannon Walters has a very badly broken wrist, thanks to your lack of self-control.' He sucks in a deep breath. 'I know you have had an enormous amount of stress to cope with over the past couple of years, Becky, being seriously ill and with your transplant. It's only because of this that I am not going to suspend you from school.'

From the corner of my eye I see Mum take a relieved breath.

'It would seem that this incident is a one-off and completely out of character, but I've talked to some of your teachers and they've reported that they've noticed a definite change of attitude in you since your return to school this term.'

I fidget uncomfortably as Mr Patterson continues his lecture.

'Mr McNamara, for example, has repeatedly found you skulking in the cloakroom when you should be in assembly and Miss Devine reports that you've refused to join in many of the group exercises in her drama class. And apparently you've only attended one PE lesson since you returned.'

'I didn't like . . . I didn't want to be . . .' My voice trails off.

'The point I am making, Becky, is that although you've certainly been through a very difficult, traumatic time, you're recovering from this now, yet over the last few weeks you've become increasingly wilful and disobedient. You appear to be a changed girl. And, unlike your former self, a girl who is not a credit to this school. How do you explain this?'

Mr Patterson and Mum stare accusingly at me, waiting for my reply. But how can I explain myself? How can I possibly tell them the truth: that I believe I am experiencing my heart donor's memories, and this is why my behaviour has changed? How can I tell them my deepest and darkest fear: that I'm taking on his whole personality?

So I bite my lip and stay silent.

Mum and I leave Mr Patterson's office and walk down the corridor in silence.

'Becky,' she asks anxiously as we reach the doors to the main entrance. 'What's happening to you?'

I hang my head as I feel her eyes burning into me. 'Nothing,' I tell her. 'I'm all right. Nothing's happening to me.'

She hesitates for a few seconds before she hurries through the doors, throwing me one last worried glance.

42

When Mum's gone I have no choice but to head back to my afternoon lessons.

Taking a deep breath, I turn the handle to the door of the science lab and walk reluctantly in.

'Come on in, Becky,' calls Mrs Williams from the front of the class as soon as she sees me. 'You're very late.'

'Sorry, miss.'

'Where have you been?'

Glancing around the class, I can tell from everyone's expressions that Mrs Williams is the only person in this room who doesn't know exactly what happened this lunchtime.

'Becky?'

'Um. Mr Patterson's office, miss.'

'Oh, I see.' Her voice alters. The sympathetic note vanishes. 'Well, you're here now. Hurry up and sit down.'

The only empty seat is between Leah and Sophie Morgan. Trying to ignore all the hostile stares, I hurry over and sink down onto the chair, wishing the ground would open and swallow me up. Sophie Morgan immediately scrapes her chair away from mine in what I suppose is an unspoken protest, and Leah doesn't look up.

'I'm really sorry, Leah, I don't know what came over me,' I whisper.

'It's not me you should be apologising to,' she hisses back.

'Shannon just pushed me over the edge —'

'It wasn't anything to do with Shannon,' she retorts.

'What do you mean?' I ask puzzled.

'It was Masher.'

'Masher?'

'Shannon didn't know anything about it.' Leah pulls a face. 'She's already got enough on her plate. They moved her to another children's home last night. Third one this year.'

'What you did was totally out of order,' snaps Sophie.

Leah raises her hand.

'Yes, Leah?' asks Mrs Williams.

'Can I move over there, please, miss?' says Leah, turning away from me and indicating the other side of the classroom. 'I can't work here.'

43

There are only a few days left until half-term, and Shannon is off school for the rest of the week. Thankfully, there are no assemblies and the weather stays dry so I still eat my lunch outside, on my own. I keep my head down and away from everyone else, which isn't hard because everyone, including Leah, stays well away from me. They've seen what happened to Shannon. No one wants to risk a confrontation with the Freak. I have nothing to do but focus on my schoolwork, so when Mum checks with McNamara on Friday, he gives me a glowing report.

'Apparently you've been working extremely hard and all your teachers are very pleased with you,' she says with a relieved smile as we're having tea.

'Sounds like things are getting back to normal,' adds Joe.

If only they knew, I think. 'Can I meet Sam tomorrow then?' I ask. We've been texting each other all week.

Mum glances at Joe, who gives a small shrug. I force a smile to disguise my irritation at him being the one who decides.

'OK,' says Mum.

'Tell him to call round here for you then I can ask him what his intentions are.'

'Joe!' Mum glances at my annoyed face.

'Only joking,' he says.

'He's just a friend, OK?' I'm glaring at him now.

'OK. Keep your wig on.' He grins infuriatingly at Mum. 'That'll be the bathroom occupied all morning then . . .'

'Mum! Tell him!'

'Joe . . . Pack it in.'

But I don't need to worry. On Saturday, both Mum and Joe are on their best non-embarrassing behaviour, and, far from interrogating Sam about 'his intentions' or any other such rubbish, Joe spends ten long and totally incomprehensible minutes in deep discussion with Sam about the highs and lows of the most recent Man United football game. I'm thinking that I'll never get Sam out of the house, but eventually Mum steps in.

'Joe,' she says, darting a knowing glance at me, 'I think that tap in the kitchen's leaking again.'

'Oh, not again . . .' he groans.

'Well. Nice to meet you, Sam,' says Mum, flashing him a smile. I can tell she approves. Ushering us both towards the front door, she adds, 'We'll see you later, Becky. Take care.'

'Thanks, Mum. Bye then.'

It's good to be with Sam again and forget about everything that has happened at school recently, but, as we near the park, I begin to feel uneasy. No matter how much I try not to think about it, what I did to Shannon keeps running through my head. The feeling builds. Finally, as we walk through the park gates, I can stand it no longer.

'Sam,' I ask tentatively, 'can I ask you something?'

'I'm not explaining the off-side rule,' he jokes.

'I'm serious,' I say.

'OK, what is it?' He's looking disconcerted now.

I take a deep breath, desperately hoping I'm not going to upset him, then plunge straight in.

'Your friend, Callum. What was he like?'

I glance over at Sam. He's staring back at me. 'What d'you mean?'

'Tell me about him.'

Sam hesitates for a second or two. 'Full of life. Clever. Funny. Fearless.' He shrugs. 'He was my best mate . . . even though he'd always borrow my homework then start telling me what I'd got wrong.' His face clouds. 'He was the brother I never had.'

We walk up to the bandstand and sit down on the wooden steps. Sam is quiet now, deep in thought.

'So, what was he into?' I ask.

'Usual boy stuff. He was annoyingly good at sport – even talent-spotted for a football academy once.'

'Wow.'

'He didn't go, though.'

'He didn't go? Why not?'

'Typical Callum. Said he liked hockey better.'

'I guess he was brilliant at that too.' I can hear my voice

and know it sounds odd. I dart a look at Sam, relieved that he hasn't noticed.

'He was amazing. Used to play for county. Their top goal scorer.'

I turn away so Sam can't see my face. 'What else?' I ask.

'He was always going on about the environment. Wouldn't eat meat.' Sam gives a small laugh. 'Used to survive on peanut butter sandwiches.'

I don't move. I don't say a word, but my mind's spinning.

'You OK?' Sam asks a few moments later.

'Um . . . yeah, course.' I say, turning back to him and forcing what I hope is a calm smile.

Down at the boating lake the herons are nesting on the little horseshoe-shaped island. Two swans swim sedately past, trailing a V of fluffy cygnets and pointedly ignoring the children throwing chunks of bread to encourage them onto the path.

'Did Callum like swans?' I ask.

'Swans?'

Perplexed, Sam thinks for a few seconds. 'Not specially. He liked all animals. Went on marches against animal cruelty and stuff like that.'

'He sounds pretty serious . . .'

'No, he was really funny. We'd be laughing all the time, although to be honest, I never knew what he was going to get up to next.'

'How do you mean?'

'Once we were in this really long, boring assembly, end of term thing. So, after ten minutes, before I could stop him, he sneaks out and no one sees him till we're all let out at breaktime. We go onto the playing field and see he's hauled all the desks out of our classroom and put them out on the grass in exactly the same positions.'

'Did he get caught?'

'Nah, he never did.'

I give a secret but huge sigh of relief. Callum sounds like he was an incredibly talented, caring but normal fifteen-year-old lad.

'We'd been friends since primary school. We were going to go backpacking when we finished school – see the whole world. But . . .' There's a note of hesitation in his voice as it trails off.

I look at him. He's frowning now.

'He changed, though. The last month of his life he was different,' he says finally.

'How?'

'Don't know. He got angry a lot. Secretive. We started arguing.'

'So what was going on?' I feel the blood draining from my face as I dread Sam's reply.

'He wouldn't tell me. I asked him. Kept asking him. But whatever it was that was eating him up, he wouldn't share it. Kept it all inside.' The bitterness in Sam's voice is growing. As much as I know this is hurting him I have to find out the truth.

'Then what happened?'

Sam shrugs and is silent for a moment. 'He started skipping lessons, then some days he just didn't turn up to school at all. The week before he died, he got suspended for fighting. That day was the last day I saw him.'

'Who was he fighting with?'

There's no answer.

'Sam. Tell me. Who was it?' I glance anxiously at him, his dark eyes fixed on the lake.

'Me,' he says finally. 'He was fighting with me.'

44

As we wander back through the park, it's as if a dark shadow has come between us. There are now three of us walking down this tarmac path. Sam, me and Callum. I fall silent, and it isn't until we reach the boating lake that Sam finally speaks.

'Becky, why d'you want to know about Callum?' he asks bluntly.

I knew this was coming, but I still feel totally unready to answer him. 'I . . . he . . . he was your friend . . .' I mutter.

Sam turns and stares at me. I can feel myself blushing. From the way his dark eyes bore into me, I know he isn't satisfied that this is the real reason. My mind is in turmoil. What should I say?

I take a deep breath and exhale slowly. 'There's something I need to tell you.'

I start to explain how I caught a virus over two years ago and how I was going to die a few months back if I didn't get a heart transplant. I tell him about the night we were summoned to the hospital, what happened before I'd gone under the anaesthetic, and how I woke up forty-eight hours later with a different heart beating inside me, and the chance of a new life ahead of me. I tell him all this and he listens without saying a single word.

When I finish, we stand side by side at the edge of the lake, staring at the still, calm surface of the water, neither one of us daring to say a thing.

And it's stupid, because I can feel tears welling up, but I can't stop them however hard I try to blink them away.

'There's more,' I say, forcing my voice to become steady. 'I know this park. I knew every corner of it, even though I've never been here until that day I first met you.'

'I don't understand.'

'I also saw you several times before we met.'

'What are you saying, Becky?'

'I'm saying, and I know this doesn't make any sense, but I'm saying, since my transplant – you . . . this park . . . other places . . . other people – I've seen them, known them, as if they've always been in my memory.'

'But how? It's not possible.'

I take another deep breath. 'They're Callum's memories.'

'Callum's?'

'I've got Callum's heart inside me.'

'Callum's heart?' Sam stares at me, dumbfounded. He shakes his head and gives a hollow laugh. 'No. No way!' He backs away from me slightly, his expression now wary.

'Callum died on October the fifteenth, didn't he?' I ask.

'How do you know that?'

'It's the same night I had my transplant.'

Sam runs his fingers through his dark hair then shakes his head in disbelief. 'No . . . this is just a coincidence. They happen all the time – they've done scientific studies. People think there's something spooky going on, but there isn't. The strange things that happen to them are literally just by chance.' His voice trails off and he falls silent.

'Sam, what's happened – is happening – to me isn't anything to do with coincidence,' I say. 'The first time I saw you was when I came round after my operation. I saw you twice more in the hospital, but I just thought you were another patient. Then, back home, I was going upstairs and there you were on the landing in front of me. You scared the pants off me. A few weeks later, I meet you in real life and find you were the best friend of a boy who died the same night I had my transplant. It's not a coincidence. We're connected by Callum.'

'I need to sit down,' Sam mutters as he sinks down onto a nearby bench. He exhales, long and deep, and then shakes his head.

'But hang on,' he says eventually, looking up at me with a troubled expression, 'even if you did have Callum's heart – and I suppose that could just be possible because he carried a donor card – how could you get his memories? A heart's just a heart. What you're telling me is impossible.'

I try to convince him. I can't bring myself to tell him about how I hurt Shannon and my fear that I might be taking on Callum's anger and aggression. So I tell him about me becoming a vegetarian and addicted to peanut butter sandwiches, painting my room and what happened when I played hockey for the first time last week. 'Sam, I don't understand it either, but this is the truth. Please believe me.'

He props his hands on his face and stares ahead, his expression darkening as he turns things over and over in his head. Finally, he looks up at me and says starkly, 'I don't know what's going on, but it's got nothing to do with Callum. It can't have and you're mad to even think it!'

45

We walk out of the park, barely exchanging a word. Sam has made it plain he doesn't believe me and I don't know what else I can do to convince him, so we say polite but awkward goodbyes and go our separate ways.

Joe's in the kitchen when I get in.

'So where's Sam the Man then?' he asks with a grin.

'Gone home,' I reply, pasting on a fake smile.

'Oh.' He glances at me as I hurry towards the door to the hallway. I can feel my smile cracking on my face but I no longer care.

'Everything OK?' he asks casually.

'I told you, we're just friends.' Or we were until today, I think bitterly.

'Oh . . . yeah,' he says gently. 'Want a cup of tea?'

'No . . . thanks.'

I run up to my room and lie down on my bed. I stare at the blue painted walls, trying to blink away the image of the house with green shutters. Finally it fades and I breathe an angry sigh of relief. I close my eyes. Although my legs ache and I feel incredibly tired, I can't stop the thoughts racing round my mind. Mum calls me down for dinner but I'm not hungry. To keep her happy I eat something, anything, but as soon as I can, I make my excuses and head back to my room.

At eleven, I switch off my light, but I can't sleep. No matter how hard I try to make sense of everything with logical, rational explanations, my thoughts twist and knot until I feel as if I am going mad.

It starts to get light and I'm still awake, listening to the birds singing outside. I glance round my room and see the sleeve of my tracksuit sticking out of my chest of drawers. Ten minutes later, I pad downstairs in my tracksuit and socks, pull on my trainers, tell Mum I'm just going for a run, then let myself out of the front door.

I first started running when I was nine, after that horrible Christmas when Dad left home and everything fell apart. I'd slip out and run and keep on running until my thoughts untangled and I felt calm again. It was worth the grief Mum gave me when I got back home. Each time, I'd run just a little further.

Then, one snowy February day, I was a couple of miles away from home, totally lost, but didn't care. I was running across a road and nearly got knocked down. The driver called the police. A policewoman took me home and I got the biggest telling off of my life, but a week later, after Mum had been up to school, my teacher put me in for an under-elevens' cross-country race. I still missed Dad, but from then on I started getting medals and trophies for running, instead of cross words.

I head down the road, walking briskly at first to warm up, then, when I reach the T- junction at the end, turn right and break into a slow jog. I'm trying hard to keep my mind off Callum, but my thoughts keep flying back to him. He'd been in trouble, truanting, fighting with Sam. My stomach churns and I feel a stab of panic. What else had he done?

I force myself to concentrate on my surroundings. Although it's early, there's plenty of traffic about. I count cars to distract myself, but it doesn't work. I'm still thinking about Callum. I increase my pace, taking longer and faster strides, trying to convince myself that any moment I'll begin to feel calm again. But instead of feeling better, I'm aware of a growing sensation of dread. Something horrible is going to happen and there's nothing I can do to stop it.

A woman passes me, staring warily as I suck in a lungful of air. I'm finding it harder and harder to breathe, my heart's thumping like a hammer and I feel I'm wrapped in a tight bandage that's being pulled tighter and tighter, squeezing every molecule of air from my lungs. My chest sears with a stabbing pain. My hands are sweaty and I'm dizzy.

The street, cars, people are becoming an unreal blur. I turn away from the road and start to stagger back along the pavement the way I came, my eyes fixed on a sign ahead. Its bright red lettering proclaims *Open seven days a week*. I've got to get home, I suddenly realise, because my heart's going to stop working any minute and, if I don't make it back, I'm going to die right here on the High Street outside Stacey's Coin-operated Launderette.

46

Somehow I manage to keep going. I make it back along our street, through the garden gate and up the path. I bang on our front door until Mum opens it.

Alarmed, she helps me inside and sits me down.

I try to speak, but she's grabbed the phone and is punching the keys. I can hear her voice trying to remain calm as she asks for an ambulance.

Three hours later, I'm sitting up on a trolley bed in the casualty department of our local hospital, wired up to a collection of monitors. Over the other side of the room, Mum is talking in hushed tones to one of the doctors who examined me. I strain to hear what they're saying, but I can only pick up fragments. Finally, they both come over. Their expressions are serious and I brace myself for the worst.

'You're fine, Becky,' says Mum, her whole body relaxing in pure relief as she reaches out and carefully hugs me through the tangle of wires.

I stare at her dumbly.

'You're OK,' she repeats, her voice cracking.

'But – I don't understand . . .'

'There's absolutely nothing wrong with your heart, Becky,' says the doctor with a smile, as she starts to detach me from one of the monitors. 'We've run the tests and all the results so far show it's working perfectly. There's no sign of rejection either.'

'Then what happened?'

She pauses for a moment then shrugs. 'We think maybe you had a panic attack. But you've no need to be anxious about your new heart. It's extremely healthy.'

'But things have been happening to me . . .' I say.

'What sort of things?' asks the doctor, peering at me over her glasses.

'I've seen things, places I've never been, people I've never met . . .' I say.

'Panic attacks are frightening. They can induce all sorts of strange symptoms. As well as the physical – your heart pounding, sweating, a choking feeling, chest pain – some people have dreamlike sensations. It's called de-realisation. It's like being in a trance; an altered state of consciousness.'

'Don't worry, Becky. You're all right,' says Mum, taking my hand in hers.

The doctor checks her notes. 'Your immunosuppressant drugs might explain a great deal about how emotional you're feeling,' she says. 'But I'm telling you again, Becky. Your heart is healthy.'

'But is it . . . a good heart?' I ask desperately.

'A good heart?' She stares at me curiously, as if the

question is out of her remit. She shrugs. 'It's a very good heart. It's strong and it's pumping well. You're incredibly lucky to have had a successful transplant. So many organs are needed and so few people sign up for the donor scheme. Every week I see people, just like you, dying for the want of a new heart. Go home, live your life and be grateful.'

47

Over the next couple of days I think long and hard about what the doctor said and realise that what she told me makes sense. I need to do what she says. I *want* to do what she says. Really I do. But somehow I just can't.

Mum talks to me about getting out and about again, seeing Leah, Jodie and Alesha. I listen and nod, but I don't tell her the real situation. Even if I still had friends, I'm not sure I'm ready to go anywhere or see anyone at the moment. So I stay in my room with just my visions for company, trying to persuade myself that I'm still me, whoever's heart I've got inside me.

Finally, I decide to text Alice. Although nothing like this has happened to her, she has been through a transplant. There's no reply to my text, so I wait an hour then ring her, but her mobile goes straight to answerphone. When my phone rings later, it's not her, it's Sam. He wants to see me. I'm confused. I don't know what to do. Part of me desperately wants to see him but I'm frightened too.

* * *

We meet at the park. Mum drops me off outside and waves to Sam, who's waiting there for me. I promise her I'll keep my phone on all the time and come home with him.

Being half-term, it's packed with kids and families out for the day in the warm spring weather. We walk up to the bandstand, neither of us speaking. I feel jittery just being outside and I wonder whether I'm doing the right thing.

'Are you OK?' he asks finally.

I nod. 'I'm fine. I'm sorry I upset you.' I say.

We sit down together and watch a bunch of small boys about Danny's age chase a ball around, and I start feeling guilty about how I treat him, always yelling and shouting at him.

Sam keeps his eyes fixed on the game, avoiding mine. 'You've got nothing to be sorry about,' Sam tells me, but I know it's not true. 'Let's walk,' he says finally, pulling me up.

We head across the park down to the boating lake, then up the path past the squishy-floored play area, avoiding the swarm of pint-sized kids playing on the swings, slides and climbing frames.

We're almost at the opposite edge of the park now. Ahead of us, I can see the iron railings and a narrow open gate.

The street on the other side is lined with tall terraced houses, three storeys high. We walk through the gate and along the street to the crossroads at the end, where there's a small corner shop.

As we approach, I see the door's open, and a tantalisingly familiar smell of spices and soap powder comes wafting out.

I drink it in, and for one moment, a sudden, inexplicable wave of happiness overwhelms all my fears.

'This way,' says Sam, throwing me a look as I hesitate by the doorway.

'Where are we going?'

'Nowhere special,' he replies with a shrug, and he leads me down the left-hand turning. But as we walk along this quieter road I realise exactly why the little shop is so familiar. And when we round the bend, I finally see it. I throw a glance at Sam, who's looking straight ahead, seemingly unaware.

'That house, there, the one with the green shutters,' I say, calmly pointing. 'Someone's changed the gate and painted the front door.'

Sam looks at me warily. 'How d'you know that?' he asks.

'Because the gate was broken and the front door used to be dark green,' I reply. 'It's Callum's house, isn't it?'

48

We walk further along the pavement towards the house. Apart from the gate and the front door, it's exactly how I've seen it in my mind's eye. I glance at Sam. His face is white as paper.

'This *is* where Callum lived, isn't it?' I hear myself saying, my heart beating fast and hard with both joy and terror.

He nods slowly and I know for sure I'm having no panic attack. This is all real.

We peer into the front garden. The daffodils are almost finished, their yellow flower heads beginning to shrivel and brown, but under the big magnolia bush I can see the green shoots of bluebells.

'I don't know what to say,' Sam whispers. 'I'm sorry. I brought you here to test you.'

'So, have I passed?'

He nods, glancing at me fearfully.

The front door to the house opens and a short, blond-haired woman of about forty appears, carrying a couple of milk bottles. As she puts them down on the step, she looks up.

'Callum's mum,' I whisper, and my heart skips a beat.

Sam nods then waves to her.

'Sam?' she calls, walking up the path towards us.

'Hi, Mrs Hunter. How are you?'

'Getting there,' she says. 'Slowly.' She tries to smile, but her eyes remain sad. 'It's so nice to see you! Come on in for a moment . . . Charley's here.'

Sam darts a look at me.

'It's OK. Bring your friend.' She turns to me, her voice trailing off. 'This used to be Sam's second home.'

49

'This is Becky,' says Sam to Callum's mum.

'Hi,' I say lamely. There are dark circles under her eyes and she looks as though she hasn't had a good night's sleep for months. A lump rises in my throat. I feel the need to say more, do more . . . and, despite my fear of germs, even hug this complete stranger who actually isn't a stranger at all.

'Hello,' she replies casually.

To her, I'm just a friend of her son's best friend. I desperately want to tell her the truth, but I know that I can't just blurt out that I'm carrying the beating heart of her dead son.

'Let's go in,' she says. 'I'll pop the kettle on.'

She ushers us into the house, through the narrow hallway, pausing at the bottom of the stairs. 'Go on into the kitchen,' she tells us, then shouts upstairs, 'Charley, Sam's here! Charley!'

As Sam and I walk into the kitchen with its scrubbed pine table and painted wooden chairs, Sam whispers to me that he hasn't been here since Callum's funeral.

Mrs Hunter bustles in. 'She'll be down in a mo,' she says, filling the kettle from the tap.

A minute later the kitchen door opens and a tall, blond girl of about eighteen appears. I instantly recognise her, but I'm still stunned to see how breathtakingly beautiful she is.

'Hi, Sam,' she says, 'how's it going?' She flashes him a smile and Sam grins broadly back. He looks like he's won the lottery.

I feel a sharp pang of jealousy. My cheeks are burning, and I glance over at Sam, hoping he hasn't noticed anything. I needn't worry. His eyes are fixed on Charley and he still has that stupid dumbstruck grin on his face.

As we all sit down, I notice that Sam, Charley and Callum's mum all avoid the blue chair. Callum's chair. I imagine him sitting there with his family in the evenings, chewing over the highs and lows of the day, chatting and laughing and bickering over a meal.

Mrs Hunter hands us mugs of tea and tentatively we begin to talk. We discuss the park, skateboarding, Sam's school and mine, Charley's A-level courses, what we all want to do when we leave school, the house . . . everything except Callum. But I know, as the four of us face each other across this table, he is the one dominating all our thoughts. It's as if he's actually here among us, lounging back invisibly on that blue chair, listening to every word we say. It would be rude to talk about him in his presence. When we finish our tea and the talk finally dries up, Mrs Hunter carries the mugs over to the sink.

'Thanks, Mrs Hunter. We'd better be going now,' says Sam, getting up.

She doesn't say anything for a second or two. Then, without turning round, she says quietly, 'Sam – there's some things of yours in Callum's room.' Her voice quivers slightly as she says Callum's name. 'Charley – show them where they all are, will you?'

'OK.'

I realise now it's too painful for her to go into her own son's bedroom. Even speaking his name is difficult. I think of the letter I tried to write to my donor's family, with its clumsy attempts to thank them and express my sadness 'at their loss'. I had absolutely no understanding until this moment how incredibly huge and shattering that loss is.

The three of us head upstairs. I know instinctively that Callum's bedroom is the one at the end of the landing on the left, but I'm not prepared for what I see when I stand at the doorway and peek in.

The room is decorated in a similar shade of pale blue to mine. His bed is underneath the window, just where I've finally moved mine. His wardrobe, chest of drawers and a desk are positioned in exactly the same places that I've put mine.

'Mum can't bear to change anything. It's just how it was the day Callum died,' says Charley, quietly. 'I suppose it still hasn't really sunk in, to be honest. I think Mum half expects him to come back home any minute.'

With a small sigh, Charley opens Callum's wardrobe and takes out a black rucksack and a battered skateboard. 'I think that's everything,' she says.

'Thanks, Charley.'

'Oh, I've got one of your CDs in my room . . .' She heads towards the door.

'Don't worry. Keep it,' says Sam, picking up the bag and skateboard. 'Is your dad around?'

Charley stops in her tracks and turns round. 'I thought you knew,' she says, staring at him. 'My parents split up last year.'

'No. I didn't know.' Sam shakes his head in bewilderment. 'I'm really sorry, Charley.'

'Dad left a few weeks before Callum died.'

'He never told me.'

'Callum refused point blank to see Dad after he'd gone. That's when he went off the rails. Truanting. Getting into trouble. Some nights he didn't come home at all.'

'Callum wouldn't tell me anything,' Sam says, 'but I knew something was wrong.'

'One morning, he came in with cuts on his face. God knows what he was getting mixed up in.' Charley frowned. 'It was like he'd pushed some kind of gigantic self-destruct button.'

50

Sam and I walk back up Callum's street in silence, both of us deep in thought. As we pass the shop, Sam speaks for the first time.

'Why couldn't he have just told me? Instead of fighting, I could have done something to help.'

'You're not to blame.'

He shakes his head and sighs. 'You don't know that. What if I could have stopped him? Kept him out of trouble.' He looks at me, suddenly realising the full implications of what he's just said. 'Oh . . . I didn't —'

'It's OK.' I blink away the tears prickling at the back of my eyes.

As we enter the park and walk across the grass to the other side, I slowly gather up the courage to ask the question that's been on my mind for months. 'What happened, Sam?' I ask. 'How did Callum die?'

'I don't know exactly. But about a week after our fight, I got a call from him out of the blue. It was late. Half-eleven

– twelve, maybe. He wasn't at home.' He shrugs. 'I don't know where he was – he wouldn't say. He was agitated though – excited – asked me to lie to his mum, to say that he was at my house if she asked. Didn't want her to worry. I pleaded with him to tell me what was going on. He said he couldn't talk any more, had to go. Then he cut me off. I tried to ring him back, but he'd turned off his phone. The following day I found out that less than an hour later, he'd been hit by a car. The driver was in shock. Said Callum had run out like crazy from nowhere and there was no way he could have avoided him. He died instantly.'

51

When we reach my house, I feel relieved that Sam says he has to get home straight away. I love being with him, but his presence is a constant reminder of Callum. I desperately need time and space to think. Get my head sorted.

I think about how Sam described the changes in Callum during the month before his death, and I remember the uncontrollable surge of anger I felt when I pushed Shannon and broke her wrist.

I can't escape it: having Callum's heart beating away inside me is changing me. His memories are affecting me. My family have noticed I'm different since my transplant. Everyone at school is aware of it. I have to face the truth about myself. For better or worse, I'm no longer the person I used to be.

But what exactly was going on in Callum's life? From what Sam and Charley said, it sounded as if he was mixed up in something really bad. Whatever it was, he must have been in way over his head.

Then I think about the night he died: he ran straight out in front of a car. Had someone been chasing him? Charley said he'd been truanting and not coming home at night. Was he mixed up in a gang? There are reports of fights and stabbings in the local newspapers every week. I feel a chill flood through me. Did Callum hurt someone, and is that why I hurt Shannon? My imagination flits from one scary scenario to another.

That night I sleep badly, tormented by a nightmare. I'm in a dark, confined space surrounded by strangers. There's no way out.

I wake suddenly and sit bolt upright, my heart pounding. I suck air into my lungs and try to reassure myself that I'm not still in that frightening place. Gradually, my eyes adjust to the lack of light and I begin to make out the familiar shapes of my things in my darkened bedroom. But even now I'm not totally convinced I'm safe. As I sit waiting for dawn, too frightened to go back to sleep, I realise the only thing I'm completely sure of is my bad heart.

52

I stare at the piece of bacon on my plate.

'Thought you didn't eat meat?' says Danny, who has wolfed down his four rashers, two eggs and a fried tomato and is now tucking into his second bowl of cereal.

'Well – maybe I've decided I do like it after all,' I reply as I tentatively push the bacon around the plate with my fork, plucking up courage to actually put it in my mouth.

Danny watches me intently. He's all kitted out in his Man United gear, ready to go to a half-term course. 'I'll have it if you don't want it,' he says. 'I'm going to need tons of energy today.'

I stab at the piece of shrivelled up flesh then force it into my mouth. 'Sorry, Squirt. Too late.'

The tangy, salty, animal taste hits my tongue immediately. Trying not to grimace, I move it around the inside of my mouth, chewing it as rapidly as I can, then swallowing it down too hastily, in one congealed lump. I can feel the pit of my stomach angrily rejecting it and I fight hard to keep it there.

'So what do you want to do today, Becky?' asks Joe, avoiding my eye as he concentrates on buttering his toast. 'Your choice. Barring trips to Florida, visits to expensive theme parks or anything involving a house full of hyperactive teenagers. I've had my orders.'

He's taken a few days off for half-term while Mum carries on working. For a moment, I can't help but wonder what Leah, Jodie and Alesha are doing this week. I've tried not to think about them over the last few days. Before I got ill, the four of us always used to hang out together in the holidays and have loads of laughs. Those days are long gone, I think bitterly.

'Well, there is something . . .' I say, finally.

'The usual retail therapy, I suppose? ' he says with a mock sigh.

'Well, sort of. I want to spend my birthday money.'

Half an hour later, we drop Danny off at the sports centre then I direct Joe out of town.

'So what exactly did you want to buy, Becky?' he asks, bemused, as we pull up outside a large DIY store.

'Paint.'

'Paint?'

'I want to paint my room and change it round again.'

'Oh, come on. Not again. You've got to be joking . . .'

'I'm not.'

'Becky, don't wind me up.' I can tell from the tone of his voice he thinks we're heading for yet another row.

'I'm not. Will you help me, Joe? Please.'

He looks at me, sees I'm deadly serious then gives a sigh and shakes his head. 'What colour this time?'

My mind goes blank; I haven't even considered this detail. 'Any,' I say eventually, 'as long as it's not blue.'

We buy a large tin of yellow paint and a couple of new rollers.

'Goodness only knows what your mum's going to say about all this,' says Joe an hour later, as he heaves all the furniture into the middle of my bedroom.

'She loves yellow,' I reply evasively.

'That wasn't what I meant and you know it,' he mutters.

We work all morning and finish just before lunchtime.

'Well,' says Joe, looking round the room. 'Was it worth it?'

I nod, breathing out a small sigh of relief. I have to untangle myself from Callum and this is one of the ways I can do it. 'Thanks.'

'We can move the furniture back in a couple of hours when it's dry,' he says.

'Great. But I don't want it all where it was before,' I say urgently.

Joe glances at me warily. 'Right. Want to tell me why not?'

I shrug and force a smile. 'I . . . I just need things to be different.'

53

Mum isn't too pleased that Joe and I have repainted my room and she tells us both off.

'At least you've done a proper job this time,' she says finally, glaring at Joe.

But her anger doesn't bother me. I'm desperate to stop thinking about Callum. I need to flush him out of my mind. If I cut out everything in my life connected to him, then just maybe I can loosen his hold on me.

Although I'm tired, I go to bed late but have another nightmare. I'm in that dark, confined space again, surrounded by strangers. This time I can feel Callum's presence. He's here with me and I'm frightened. I must be yelling in my sleep, because the next thing I know I open my eyes to see Mum.

'Becky, it's all right. You're OK.'

I peer around the room. Everything is as it should be yet I still feel this horrible sense of impending danger.

'You were dreaming, Becky. Just dreaming,' says Mum,

stroking my hair. 'I told Joe it wasn't a good idea for you to sleep in this room for a day or two. There's still a paint smell. I'm not surprised you were having a nightmare.'

But the smell of paint has nothing to do with it. I'm sure that somehow I have to do more to disconnect myself from Callum, to cut away as many links to him as I can. There'll be no more trips to the park. And somehow I'm going to have to try to blank out the visions of his memories.

I know what else I have to do but it takes me all the next morning to pluck up the willpower to do it.

'Sam?' I sit on the stairs holding the phone to my ear, dreading the sound of his voice.

'Hey, Becky!' he replies and my heart misses a beat. I really don't want to do this.

'What you up to?' he asks.

'Not much.' I desperately want to delay the moment for as long as possible.

'Me neither . . . Want to meet up?'

I take a deep breath, shut my eyes then force myself to say the lines I've been rehearsing for the last three hours. I can hear my voice – wooden and unreal as if it belongs to someone else.

'Sam. I'm sorry, I can't see you today . . .'

'Oh.' He sounds disappointed. 'Saturday, then?'

'No. I can't.'

There's a pause down the line, then he says, 'You OK? You sound upset.'

I try to reply but my voice won't obey me. No words come out.

'Becky?' he asks again. 'What's wrong?'

'I'm sorry,' I blurt out. 'I can't see you on Saturday or any other day. I'm not going to see you again.'

'But . . . I thought . . . we . . .' his voice trails away. 'Why?'

'I just can't.' Tears well up in my eyes.

'You got another boyfriend or something?'

Another *boyfriend*? I feel a short-lived stab of joy as I realise he feels we're more than just friends. I want to tell him right here and now that I feel the same. But I don't. Instead I make myself repeat like a stupid robot, 'I'm sorry I can't see you again.'

'What have I done?' He sounds really upset. I'm hurting him and I hate myself for it.

'Nothing.' I reply quickly. 'You haven't done anything.'

'Then what's wrong?' He waits for my answer.

'It's Callum,' I say finally.

'What do you mean, Callum?'

'I don't want to know anything else about him or what happened to him.'

'Well . . . we don't have to talk about Callum.' His voice sounds hoarse. 'I don't understand.'

'He's always here between us. It's you, me . . . and him. I can't handle it any more. I'm sorry —' I bite my lip to try to stop the tears that are rolling down my face.

'Becky —'

'I've got to go now . . . Sam, I'm so sorry.' I don't wait to hear his reply. I put down the phone feeling completely and utterly desolate.

54

Knowing I'm never going to see Sam again is pretty much like the end of everything, but I still manage to convince myself that this is the only way to break free from Callum.

Although neither Mum nor Joe say anything to me about Sam, they both know something has happened.

'Why don't you give Leah a call?' Mum suggests. 'Get her round for the evening if she's not over at her auntie's. We've got that new DVD and I'll make you some popcorn.'

'No, thanks, Mum.'

'Gran said Jake's mum told her that a whole bunch from your class are going ice-skating tomorrow evening,' she persists. 'You could go too.'

No, I really couldn't, I think. No one from my class would want me with them after what happened with Shannon. But I don't tell Mum this.

In the end, I retreat to my room and spend the evening trying not to think about either Sam or Callum.

My head's hurting with the effort of it all, and I feel so

worn out that I go to bed at nine. I sleep badly, as both Sam and Callum continue to haunt me in dark and frightening dreams. I haven't managed to escape either of them.

It must be late in the morning when Danny charges into my room.

'Aren't you ever getting up?' he yells.

'No . . .' I mutter, my head pounding and my whole body aching. It's too much effort to try and look at the clock or him so I don't move. My throat has closed up as if I've swallowed a sheet of sandpaper.

'Come on, Becky – we're going to Gran's in half an hour.'

I groan and roll over.

'Mum,' I hear Danny call, 'Becky says she's not ever getting up.'

'Don't be daft, Danny,' I hear her reply.

She comes into the room, takes one look at me, feels my forehead with her incredibly cool fingers then disappears. She reappears seconds later, holding a thermometer, which she gently pops into my mouth. I'm too tired to object. After a while, she takes it out and peers at it. I can tell by her frown it isn't good news.

'A hundred and two,' she says, stroking my hair back away from my face. 'I'm going to ring Dr Sampson's secretary.'

Two hours later, I'm lying on a bed in an outpatients' room at the hospital, wired up and undergoing a battery of tests. A nurse has already taken at least a gallon of blood and is hovering like a vampire, ready to take more. Dr Sampson is explaining to Mum that they're going to keep me in, just to be on the safe side.

'Don't worry, Becky,' Mum tells me, her face white, 'everything's going to be just fine.'

'What's happening?'

She hesitates before she speaks. 'They think you might have an infection.'

From then on, things start to get hazy. It seems that I'm being constantly poked and prodded, when all I want is to shut my eyes and go to sleep.

'We just have to get the balance right,' I hear a nurse telling Mum. 'Too much and they'll lower the levels of the immunosuppressants, and we don't want that . . .'

Even in my semi-conscious state, I don't need to ask why. I know that, without my immune system being suppressed, my body will start to reject my heart.

55

I don't remember much about the next few days. There are vague things I can recall – but whether I'm dreaming or they're real, I can't tell. Often, Mum is at my bedside, asleep or reading, then seconds later, before I can say anything, she'll be replaced by Joe. It's annoying the way people come and go so speedily. Why can't they just stay still for a minute or two? What's the rush?

Over the continual beeping, sometimes there are voices – calm, businesslike mumblings that run over me like a stream burbling over pebbles. People call my name, but never seem interested in waiting long enough for me to answer. Once or twice I do try to reply, but I'm shocked to discover that my body no longer seems to belong to me. It's merely a container for my thoughts, a hollow shell that has no ability to do as I ask.

Time is running on different tracks, it no longer obeys normal rules but enjoys doing its own thing and confusing the hell out of me. I'm sure at one point I see Sam, standing behind the partition glass looking in at me. I definitely must be dreaming – I've treated him so badly, he's the last person I deserve to see . . . but the one I most desperately want. If only I could reverse time, and take back what I said. Make things right again.

And then, without warning he's gone. I'm plunged into complete darkness, and find myself drifting alone in a great black space, a universe without stars. All hope has vanished. I'm everywhere and nowhere. The emptiness is suffocating and yet I know I have chosen it. This is where I wanted to be.

As I float on endlessly, a tiny and insignificant speck of dust in the vast and overwhelming darkness, I hear a voice, clearly and distinctly speak directly to me.

'Everything's spangles,' it says.

56

'It's good to see you, Becky.'

I force my eyes open and, blinking through heavy lashes, see Dr Sampson standing by the side of my bed.

He smiles. 'That was a pretty close call, young lady,' he says quietly. 'You had us all a little worried for a while.'

Mum steps forward. 'How are you feeling, Becky?' she asks.

I give her the edited version. 'Not brilliant.'

'Your body's had a very good attempt at rejecting your new heart, but I think we've managed to get things under control . . . for now,' says Dr Sampson. 'It'll be a few more days before you feel back to normal, but thankfully, you're on the mend.'

I do start to feel better, but I still have to stay in hospital for the rest of the week. Joe says it's a shame that I'm missing school and 'all my friends', but to be honest it's a huge relief not to be going back for a while.

The following day, the nurses encourage me to get up and walk around. I wander down the corridor, past the battered vending machine where Alice and I bought hot chocolate drinks. The machine has an out of order sign slapped on it. Typical. I smile and think about Alice, deciding she's probably out on her favourite horse right now, galloping merrily through some field or other.

I turn to go and see Natalie come out of the playroom with a small pale-looking boy.

'Well, you certainly look a lot better!' she says, a huge grin spreading over her face. I give a little shrug.

'I feel better,' I tell her, realising that for once I'm not making this up.

'That's great. You'll be home before you know it.'

'How did Alice get on?' I ask. 'She was itching to get out of the asylum, last time I saw her. I've tried texting and ringing her, but she hasn't replied.'

Natalie glances at me then turns to the little boy. 'Go and get that story you wanted and I'll come and read it to you in a minute . . .' she tells him, and he pads back into the playroom.

'Alice didn't make it, Becky,' says Natalie softly.

'What d'you mean?' I ask, blankly.

'We discovered she needed another heart but there wasn't one available. We tried to keep her going in the hope we'd get a donor.' Natalie takes my hand and holds it gently. 'She died in hospital just over a week ago.'

I stare at her in complete shock. 'No. That can't be right,' I say, forcing a small laugh. 'Not Alice . . . What about her riding? She was going to be a riding instructor. It was all planned. She told me.'

'Dr Sampson did everything he could but we ran out of time.'

It takes the whole day for what Natalie said to fully sink in. Alice was so full of life, it seems totally impossible she could die. The last time we met, she told me they were repeating her tests. I wonder if she knew then that she was in trouble, and the grin on her face masked how she was really feeling.

Tears well up in my eyes as I think how Alice lived every single second of the extra time she was given. I can't say the same about me.

It's late. As I lie in the hospital bed, I make a vow that things are going to be different from now on. I've just had a very close shave but, unlike Alice, I've survived. I've been given another chance. And then it dawns on me. The only way I'm ever going to be able to truly live my life is if I face my fears. All of them. And that means finding out the truth about Callum.

57

'Sam . . . it's me . . . Becky.'

I can hear the tremor in my voice and I grip the phone tighter. What if he won't speak to me? Doesn't want anything more to do with me? It's no more than I deserve, I think bitterly. I shut my eyes, anticipating the worst.

'Becky?'

I try to analyse the tone of that one word. Is he angry?

'Are you still at the hospital?'

Not anger. Fear.

'No . . . I'm home.'

He knows? But how?

I force my voice to sound normal. 'I got home a few days ago.' And I've been thinking about you every single minute since, I want to add, but don't.

'I came round your house last week – your little brother told me where you were. I went to see you but they wouldn't let me in.'

My heart leaps a beat. He cares.

'Are you OK now?'

'Yes. I'm back at school on Monday.' I take a deep breath. He cares, but is it too late? Have I already hurt him too much? Have I ruined everything? 'I'm so sorry.' A lump forms in my throat.

There's a long pause. I get ready to say a brief goodbye and to put down the phone.

'I've missed you,' I hear him say, finally.

The lump in my throat melts like ice cream on a hot summer's day. Suddenly I'm floating on air. 'I've missed you too.'

'They said you'd nearly died.'

The line goes quiet.

'Sam?'

'Sorry . . . I was just . . .' He gives a forced laugh. 'First Callum . . . then you . . . I don't think I could have . . . if you had . . .' His voice trails away to nothing.

'I'm here. I'm alive. It's OK,' I say.

'I've got to see you. So I believe it,' he whispers. And although I can't see his face, I know he's crying.

A few hours later on this sunny, Saturday morning, I'm sitting in the garden with him, being spied on by Danny, but not caring one little bit.

'I need to know what happened to Callum the night he died,' I say quietly.

'Is finding out really going to make everything OK, though?' he asks, his dark brown eyes staring into mine.

'I don't know,' I reply. 'Maybe it won't. Part of me is

scared stiff to even try.'

'You mean in case he was involved in something bad?'

'Remember that old black and white film about the doctor who drank some potion and changed?' I ask.

'*Dr Jekyll and Mr Hyde.*'

'That's how Callum appears to me. One minute, he's an ordinary lad who loves sport and won't eat bacon butties, and the next, he's some kind of monster, picking fights and mixed up in goodness knows what.'

'Hang on . . . he was my friend, OK?'

'You said yourself he changed.' I sigh. 'I need to find out for myself what was going on, because I've got his heart inside me. If what I learn is bad, I have to confront it and deal with it, rather than let it eat away at me all the time.'

'But how are you going to deal with something like that?'

'I don't know, but I can't live like this any more, Sam. I have to know the worst, whatever it is.'

He's quiet for a moment. I glance over at Danny, who's peeping out from behind a tree trunk, playing with some binoculars he's made from a couple of cardboard tubes and half a reel of sticky tape.

'I'll help you,' says Sam at last. 'We'll do this together.'

58

We lie on the grass side by side, talking. Although the sun feels hot on my face, and I'm wearing a T-shirt underneath, I don't want to take off my high-necked jumper and reveal my scar.

'But how are we going to get any answers?' I ask Sam. 'Callum died nearly five months ago.'

Sam gives a shrug, then sweeps his hair off his forehead. His dark eyes glint with the hint of an idea. 'You've seen things,' he says finally. 'You've seen and felt Callum's memories. Maybe that's our key.'

I feel a shiver run up my back to the top of my neck. 'But I can't summon up things at will. His memories just appear when I'm not expecting them. Out of the blue.'

'Try.'

'What?'

'Try to imagine yourself as Callum on the night he died. Where was he? What was he doing?'

'OK, I'll give it a go.' I take a deep breath to steady my

nerves. My stomach is churning – I'm terrified of what I might see. I close my eyes. For a few moments there's nothing. I concentrate harder, but all I can hear is the traffic from the main road, and the man who lives three doors down, hammering in his shed.

I open my eyes. 'This isn't going to work,' I tell Sam. 'I can't see anything.'

'Keep trying,' he urges.

I'm about to shut my eyes again when I see Danny watching us through those daft loo-roll tubes.

'What you doing?' he asks curiously.

'Nothing. Just talking.'

I think he'll go away, but he creeps nearer and then sits down quietly behind us. He takes a small toy car out of his jeans pocket and starts pushing it round the grass, occasionally eyeing us when he thinks we aren't looking.

'Try again,' Sam tells me.

I shut my eyes and wait. Again I can see nothing. An aeroplane flies overhead and the man in his shed starts drilling. I can hear Danny making car noises as he pretends to play nearby. It's hopeless. Frustrated, I'm about to open my eyes when suddenly, emerging from the swirling colours behind my eyelids, I can see a shape forming.

'Sam . . . I can see something.'

'What is it?'

I shut out all external noises and focus inwards.

'It's . . . a circle.' I'm sure now. 'A red circle.'

'OK,' says Sam, 'keep concentrating. Give yourself a chance.'

I try my best but the image is fading.

'I don't know . . . there's a line too. A blue line,' I say, desperately trying to visualise more.

'What else?'

I'm back to blackness. I shake my head.

'Nothing. That's all.'

'It doesn't make sense.'

'A red circle and a blue line. It doesn't mean anything,' I say, disappointed.

Danny stops pushing his car on the grass and looks over at us. 'Yes it does,' he says.

We turn to him and see his freckled face and clear blue eyes staring back at us earnestly.

'It's the underground sign.'

I look at him and slowly realise he's right. 'Danny, you're a genius!' I say, impulsively reaching out to give him a hug.

'I know,' he replies with a grin, before strolling up the path to the house.

Sam turns to me. 'Can you remember anything else?'

I close my eyes and concentrate again. 'Nothing. Except that underground logo.'

'So, if Callum was on a tube train the night he died, that's where we've got to start,' he says, suddenly getting to his feet.

'What d'you mean "start"?' I ask nervously.

'We've got to try and recreate his journey. Then maybe you'll remember more.'

I can feel the blood draining from my face as I think of the hordes of bodies in the confined space of a tube station.

Hundreds of people carrying a multitude of germs. My worst nightmare.

'I . . . I don't think I can do it.'

Sam looks at me, puzzled. 'But you're better now, aren't you?' he asks. 'You said you were going back to school on Monday and everything.'

'It's not that.' I sigh. 'I've got this thing about being in crowded places. I can't cope with them. I get really panicky.'

There's an awkward silence.

'So that's why you never wanted to get a bus or tube to the park . . . I thought you just liked walking.'

I hang my head. 'I didn't want to tell you the real reason.'

'I would have understood.'

'Then please don't ask me to do this.'

'But if you don't, you're never going to find out what happened that night,' says Sam urgently. 'It's our only clue.'

59

I toss and turn all that night, thinking about what to do. I know Sam is right. The only hope I have of finding out what really happened to Callum is to try to retrace his steps – but I'm petrified. By the time I'm dressed the following morning, I've come to a decision. Before I can change my mind, I text Sam to tell him I'll meet him at the park at ten, then I cadge a lift from Joe, who's taking Danny to football practice.

'You sure you're feeling OK, Becky?' Joe asks, as we drop Danny off at his practice ground.

'I'm fine. Really. Don't worry. Just need a bit of fresh air.'

Despite my protestations, he insists on my staying with him in the car until we see Sam coming along the street.

'Thanks for the lift,' I say, hopping out of the car.

'You mind how you go . . . Stay with Sam,' he calls after me.

'Don't worry, I will!' I reply, as I walk through the park gates and hurry over to Sam.

Sam takes my hand in his and holds it gently. 'Don't be afraid,' he says quietly. 'I'll be with you all the time.'

I give his hand a small squeeze and we head across the park, down past the still water of the boating lake and up to the gate on the opposite side. I think about the monster fish lurking beneath the surface and wonder if he's still there.

We walk along the street to the crossroads where the little shop sits low and squat between two elegant terraces. Then, instead of turning left into Callum's road, we go straight on for about a hundred metres, till we see the underground sign ahead of us.

'Ready?' asks Sam.

'Yeah,' I say, tightening my grip on his hand. 'Let's go.'

60

We walk together into the tube station foyer. I glance around nervously. There are a few people milling about, but it reassures me slightly to see that the place is pretty empty. We head over to the ticket machine and study the tube map on the wall.

'So where do we go?' Sam asks, turning to me.

As I scan the different stations, I try to weigh up whether one seems more important than any other, but nothing jumps out at me.

'I don't know,' I reply with a bewildered shrug.

In the end we buy all-day travelcards. We go through the barrier and make our way down a winding tunnel until we reach an escalator, which I know will plunge us down into the depths of the station.

'OK?' asks Sam.

I'm not, but I nod as confidently as I can.

As we step onto the escalator and ride down on its silver grilled steps, a sooty draught blasts up at us and makes me shiver. I can hear the distant rumblings of trains travelling deep beneath us. I feel for Sam's hand and hold it tightly. He turns back to me and gives a reassuring smile, but he looks different – the pale fluorescent lighting has sucked the colour from his skin.

At the bottom of the escalator we are confronted by two tunnels, snaking off in opposite directions. As we stand between them, trying to decide which one to take, a crowd of people comes flooding out from the left-hand tunnel, surging around us. Seconds later, more people emerge from the other tunnel. Over the tannoy, a voice is spouting something about 'unavoidable delays'.

'Sam?' I say, looking at him fearfully.

'Let's go,' he replies, and we start to weave our way down the second tunnel through the mass of people. I just manage to cling onto his hand until we get to the platform, but then we become separated by a few metres.

'Go further along the platform,' Sam calls to me urgently. 'We'll get on the next train . . .'

I try to catch him up, but two women pushing buggies come between us and I just can't get past them. 'Sam – wait!' I call.

A train is pulling in now. Its doors swish open and, as people flood out, others surge forward, ready to climb on. Sam is about three metres away from me now. As he steps onto the train, people surge in front of me, filling the carriage and forcing Sam further down inside.

Before I can get any nearer, the doors to the carriage snap shut. For a few brief seconds, I catch a glimpse of Sam's horrified face staring out at me from behind the grubby window, then I watch the train move slowly off, until it's swallowed completely by the darkness of the tunnel ahead.

61

I spin around, wondering what to do. The platform is still crowded and I desperately feel the urge to run for the exit, to get right out of this dark cave and back up into the sunshine outside. But I force my feet to remain planted where they are. Within a couple of minutes, a second train draws up at the platform. I figure that Sam will get out at the next station and wait for me there. All I have to do, I tell myself, is to get on this train, then get out at the next stop and rejoin him.

But this is easier said than done. Even if I manage to summon up the courage to follow my plan, the train in front of me is packed. I glance around the busy platform. How on earth are all these extra bodies going to fit in there too, I wonder, as my heart starts to thump faster.

The doors to the carriages swish open and several passengers get out, then everyone surrounding me suddenly surges forward. Caught in the moving tide of people, I nervously edge towards the nearest carriage entrance, then take two more small steps and find myself inside the train.

I planned to stay as close to the doors as I can, but I'm carried deeper inside until I'm standing in the middle of the carriage between two facing rows of seats. The hot air smells stale. I cover my nose and mouth with my hand, in the hope that I can somehow avoid breathing in anything bad. The doors at each end of the carriage are wide open. I can still get off. But within seconds they swish shut and it's too late. There's no escape now.

The train lurches away from the platform. I can't bear to hold onto anything, so I immediately fall sideways.

'Sorry,' I mumble stupidly into the back of a grey overcoat, whose owner doesn't reply. Reluctantly, I reach my left arm above me and fix my hand around the handrail, which is coated, I know, with layers of invisible bacteria from the hundreds of hands that have touched it previously. It can't be long until we get to the next stop, I try to reassure myself, as the carriage lurches and rattles its way through the dark tunnel.

With each passing second, I become more and more aware of a thick, choking sensation building in my throat. My skin prickles hot and cold, my heart is racing. I lower my head and stare at the floor, which seems to be moving up and down. My whole body feels unsteady and weak – I'm getting giddy. Desperately I look up and fix my eyes on a single spot on the ceiling of the carriage. Just a few more seconds, I tell myself over and over again. I just have to hang on for a tiny bit longer and I'll make it.

But then something unexpected happens. The train grinds to a halt, its brakes squealing. We're all jolted forward and I fight hard to stay on my feet. Outside, there is nothing but darkness. We've stopped in the middle of nowhere. There are low resigned groans and irritated mutters from people around me, followed by a subdued silence as everyone waits for something to happen.

A few minutes later, without warning, all the lights go out. The whole train is plunged into pitch black. There are gasps and a small child at the far end of the carriage starts to wail uncontrollably. Near to me I can hear the anxious voices of a French couple.

Then an elderly lady's voice calls out, 'Something terrible must have happened.'

As the long minutes pass, and no lights come back on, rumours of fires and bomb attacks start to spread around the carriage. Moment by moment, the air in the carriage feels hotter, stifling. Unbearable. A man near me mutters that he has to get out. Further down the carriage, I can hear someone banging on a window.

Then, just when I think I can't bear it any longer, out of the darkness and the chaos around me, I suddenly hear a voice I recognise.

Someone clearly says, 'Everything's spangles.'

It's the same voice I heard in the hospital, the night I almost died. The voice that, until this moment, I was sure belonged to one of the nurses. A wave of relief washes over me, and I hear myself calling loudly into the blackness surrounding me, 'Please, everyone . . . there's no need to be frightened!'

To my surprise, the whole carriage slowly quietens. Even the little toddler at the far end hushes.

'Everything is going to be all right.'

62

Within seconds, the lights in the carriage come on again, and everyone peers around, blinking and half-dazed by the harsh fluorescent glare. Feelings of relief are visible on people's faces, and a self-conscious cheer goes up from a group of lads bunched in the far corner. Perhaps it's just me, but everyone seems to be smiling.

Finally, the train starts moving again. As we pull into the station some minutes later, I peer through the window, searching for Sam. There's no sign of him. The platform is empty, except for a group of Japanese tourists trundling suitcases behind them. The carriage doors open and people start getting off the train.

I'm about to follow, when something stops me in my tracks. I don't see or hear anything – I just have an incredibly strong feeling that this isn't the right place. Callum's journey isn't over here. I turn around and go and sit down on one of the now empty seats.

A little boy of about two sits down next to me followed

by a girl. It's Leah. We stare at each other in shock. Neither of us speaks for a moment. The little boy kneels on the seat beside me and bounces a small plastic dinosaur along the shelf behind. I realise he is the toddler who was so frightened earlier.

'My little brother, Ben,' Leah says finally.

'Last time I saw him he wasn't even walking,' I reply.

We sit side by side, in total embarrassment. Shyly, the little boy smiles up at me. I smile back.

'I was petrified when all the lights went out,' Leah says quietly.

'Me too.'

'Everything all right,' says the little boy.

'Was that you, Becky?' asks Leah. 'I thought I recognised your voice.'

I nod.

We pull into a station. Leah picks up Ben and stands up.

'I'm getting off here. Got to drop Ben off at my auntie's. Dad's working all next week. Where are you going?'

'Um . . . I'm not sure.'

'You OK?'

'Yeah, don't worry. I'm fine. Really.'

We wait awkwardly for the doors to open.

'See you back at school, then.'

I look up at her. 'Bye.'

'You take care,' she says, looking me straight in the eye.

'And you.' I watch her get off the train and walk up the platform as the train moves off.

I look around the carriage and recognise the voice of the

old lady who thought something terrible had happened. She's talking to the young lad next to her. At the other end of the carriage, the man in a grey overcoat is offering a bottle of water to the French couple.

As we travel on, I gradually become aware that this is what Callum was doing when he went off on his own. He was riding the tube trains all day. And then I realise the truth. I no longer have my own heart, I have someone else's. I'll be connected to him for as long as I live, just as he is connected to me – but I'm not afraid of that any more.

I look around at my fellow travellers and realise that our carriage, trundling along on the rails beneath us, is just one of hundreds, each full of people whose stories interweave as they journey through life. And no matter how hard we may try to go it alone, it doesn't work – we still need one another, as we all hurtle through space on the same crowded planet.

63

The train pulls into the next station, my heart misses a beat and I know this is where I have to get off. I step out of the carriage and make my way through the gloomy tunnel. I hurry up the escalator and rush out of the station into the stark sunshine, then quickly text Sam and tell him I'm OK.

I have no idea where I am, but this isn't going to stop me. Turning left, I start running along the street, dodging passers-by, ignoring their wary looks. The soles of my trainers strike the pavement with a satisfying thudding sound, and I give in to the urge to run faster and faster. Soon I'm sprinting flat out like a shot from a gun, and my heart is beating fit to burst. But I feel no fear. No panic. I'm totally exhilarated. The last time I felt like this was approaching the finishing tape at the cross-country race I won a few days before I got ill.

The enormity of what Callum has done for me hits me now with a force that stuns me. He thought beyond himself, his own life, his own death and reached out to help a fellow human being. Someone he'd never even met. He's given me the precious gift of new life. How on earth could I have wasted so much time already?

Out of the blue, a sharp pain stabs into my heart and stops me dead in my tracks. As I rub my chest, trying to ease it, I glance around confused.

Then I see them. On the opposite pavement, leaning against the foot of a lamp-post are the withered remnants of a bunch of flowers. As I cross the road, I know this is where Callum died. I feel overwhelmed by sadness, but there's something stronger gnawing at me too. A terrible yearning. I'm still not at the right place. Something inside me insists that Callum wasn't being chased the night he died. He wasn't mad or bad, and he hadn't been running away from anything. He was running *towards* something.

He'd been so desperate to get to his destination that he wasn't looking, and he'd run out in front of a car. His death had been a terrible event that he hadn't seen coming. Just like my infection and Alice's heart failing, bad, unfair things sometimes happen. But because of Callum's death, I'm now alive. Unwittingly, he's saved me and I'm totally and utterly grateful. And now, I realise I need to do something for him in return.

64

I start walking. I have no idea where I'm going, but this is a minor detail. I just need to get there. I thread my way through the back streets. At one point, I'm about to take a right turning, but hesitate, then take the opposite turning. The one I somehow know is correct.

Ten minutes later, I stop in front of a pub. Its door is half open, and the smell of beer and cooked food comes wafting out. Puzzled, I look up, then give a surprised gasp. Painted on the sign hanging over the pavement is a white swan – the name of the pub. I know I've arrived. I'm finally in the right place.

I step inside. The room is almost empty. There's just one old man in the corner, nursing a mug of beer and the landlord standing behind the bar polishing a glass.

'Yes, love?' asks the landlord.

I stand here not knowing what to do or say.

'Cat got your tongue?' the old man sniggers.

'Callum Hunter . . .' I say hesitantly.

'Callum Hunter?' The landlord looks puzzled. '*Nick* Hunter, you mean?'

'Um. Yes . . . is he here?'

'Out the back. I'll give him a shout. You'd better wait outside – you're underage, love . . . Nick, someone here for you!' he calls as I scurry back outside and wait. Seconds later, a man appears. I feel I know him.

'Who are you?' he asks.

'My name's Becky Simmons.'

'Do I know you?' He's frowning now.

'No. But I need to tell you something.'

'Oh yeah . . . tell me what?'

'Callum —'

His face suddenly changes. 'What about Callum?' he demands. 'Look, love, if this is some kind of wind up, I don't need it, all right?'

He turns and is almost back through the pub door. I have to say something, quickly. 'I need to tell you that . . . that . . . everything's spangles —' I blurt out.

He stops and turns to face me. His eyes search my face and meet mine. 'Say again?' he says suspiciously.

'Everything . . . is . . . spangles?'

He glares at me. I can feel myself blushing.

'I'm sorry. It's just . . .' My voice trails away as I notice the tears welling up in his eyes.

'That's what Callum used to say,' he says quietly. 'Every time we'd had an argument. "Everything's spangles, Dad," he'd say, and then I knew our bust-up was over and everything was all right.' He wipes his face with the palm of his hand. 'It was our code. No one else knew about it – not even his mum.' He stops and stares at me. 'So how on earth do you know that and what do you want?'

I take a deep breath before I speak. 'I had a heart transplant the night Callum died. I've got his heart and . . . I wanted to say thank you to your son for giving me my life back.'

65

We talk for over an hour. Callum's dad wants to know everything, and so I describe as well as I can the visions and memories that have become such a big part of my life since my transplant. I tell him about going to the park and meeting Sam, and about hearing Callum's voice at the hospital and on the tube train. Most importantly of all, I tell him that I'm sure Callum wanted to see him that night.

'When his mum and I split up, I tried and tried but he just wouldn't see me,' he says. 'Wouldn't even talk on the phone. He hated me.'

'No. He loved you,' I say firmly.

'Charley phoned me late that night. When I got to the hospital, he was already dead.' He gives a long, deep sigh. 'They let me see him. He was just lying there . . . peaceful. But I was too late . . .' He looks up at me, haunted. 'I was too late.'

'I know Callum loved you, because that's why he was coming to see you that night. He desperately wanted to make everything all right again between you both. He just never arrived.'

Callum's dad hides his eyes behind his hand. It's a few seconds before he speaks. 'We knew he'd signed up for the donor scheme a couple of years ago, but we never thought . . . He was just a kid! But when the doctors talked to his mum and me about taking his heart to save someone else's life, there was no way we were going to refuse. We both knew it was what Callum wanted. He was a good lad. The best.'

66

Callum's dad takes me back to the tube station and we say goodbye. As I make my way down the escalator and back onto a train, I realise I'm not frightened any more. I'm thinking about Callum and his family. Before I know it, I'm stepping out of the tube station near to the park. Sam's standing at the entrance waiting for me.

'Are you okay?' he asks anxiously, as he hurries over and hugs me. His arms feel warm and safe.

'I'm fine. Really.' And for the first time in two years, I actually mean it.

'I got out at that next station and waited for ages . . . but you never came. What happened?'

We walk back through the park and sit on a bench at the far corner of the lake. It's warm in the sunshine and it feels good to be sitting by the water. I start telling Sam everything that happened since we got separated.

'So Callum really spoke to you?' he asks quietly.

'I don't know. It was strange. It was as if I could hear his voice inside my head, and it calmed me down. And from that moment on everything felt different. I knew I didn't need to be afraid any more.'

When I finish my story, I can see Sam is struggling to take it all in. He looks up and stares at me, his puzzled eyes searching my face. Then his expression changes; his eyes widen and he takes a sudden sharp in-breath.

'What is it?' I ask.

He hesitates, then slowly says, 'Do you think all this could be like . . . well like . . . destiny or something?'

I look at him blankly. 'What do you mean?'

He shakes his head. 'Something happened years ago. I don't know . . . Callum. Callum told me about this girl he'd seen. I can picture him now, going on about her. I remember him insisting there was something about her. She was special, he said. She was special. But he couldn't explain what he meant and I didn't understand at the time.' He frowns slightly and his voice slows. 'We were only about ten, and he'd been on his way home from some hockey match with his team. She'd nearly got run over by the minibus they were in.'

My heart slips a beat. 'What did she look like?' I ask, hardly daring to breathe.

'Long, dark hair, a pale face and the saddest expression he'd ever seen.'

I meet Sam's eyes, remembering the small, dark-haired girl I'd seen crying in the snow. A lump rises in my throat. Of course I knew who she was . . . who she is. I just hadn't realised until now.

'It was me,' I tell him. 'That little girl Callum saw was me.'

'I knew it,' Sam whispers.

'I'd run off . . . my dad had left home a few weeks before. I missed him like crazy. It was like the end of my world.'

Sam takes a long, slow breath then exhales. 'So you did meet Callum.'

I cast my mind back all those years. I remember standing in the snow, looking up at the minibus that almost killed me and seeing the face of a young boy staring out through the window, meeting my eyes, holding my gaze.

'Yes. . . that was him.' A shiver goes right through my body. 'We did meet . . . before.'

Sam takes my hand and cradles it in his, and we sit side by side, by the edge of the lake, thinking about Callum.

Suddenly the water a few feet away begins to bubble. We stare into the lake as a huge fish surfaces and begins to gulp flies out of the air.

'It's him, it's the old monster,' says Sam with a small laugh.

We watch in silence for several minutes as the fish suns himself close to the water's surface. His wet scales glisten in the sunshine like polished diamonds.

'He's beautiful.' I whisper.

Then, without warning, there's an elegant flip of a tail, a small delicate splash and he's gone. The surface of the lake returns to its former glassy smoothness.

I turn back to Sam. 'There's something I have to do,' I tell him. 'Will you come with me?'

67

We make our way along Callum's road to his house and knock on the door. His mum answers. She looks surprised to see us.

'Mrs Hunter, can we come in for a moment?' I ask quietly.

'Of course,' she replies.

We go inside and sit down around her kitchen table.

'Is Charley home?' I ask.

'She's upstairs . . .'

'Would you call her?'

'Yes . . . OK,' Callum's mum looks from Sam to me, with a bewildered expression on her face. 'Charley!'

Callum's sister appears. 'Hiya . . . what you doing here? Sam, you're too late if you want that CD back – I've lent it to my boyfriend,' she says, flashing Sam a smile.

'No, that's cool,' Sam replies, looking at me. 'Becky needs to talk to you both.'

They turn to me, surprised.

It isn't easy, but as gently as I can, I tell them about my transplant and how I know it was Callum's heart that I received.

'That is . . . amazing,' says Charley with a dumbfounded look on her face. 'Totally . . . amazing!'

'He saved my life.'

I turn to Callum's mum. She's looking down and hasn't said a single word since I began my story. Have I done the right thing in telling her, I suddenly wonder? She was devastated by Callum's death. The last thing I want to do is upset her more.

'Mrs Hunter . . . maybe I shouldn't have told you all this – I'm really sorry.'

After a few seconds, she raises her head and looks straight at me with those sad, tired eyes. I feel terrible. What have I done?

Slowly she reaches out her hand. 'Do you mind?' she asks, her voice shaking slightly.

I shake my head. The palm of her hand gently touches my T-shirted chest. She closes her eyes and smiles as she feels the beating of her son's heart.

68

That afternoon, when I get home, it's as if a huge weight has been lifted off me. I spend some time in the garden with Danny, being goalie as he kicks his football around. The ball gets muddy and pretty soon there's dirt on my hands, but as I rub them together, I realise it's OK. It doesn't matter. Danny's surprisingly good and, when I tell him, his little face lights up.

'Becky, how long is five kilometres?' he asks as he scores yet another goal past me.

'Not that far, Squirt. About here to Gran's. Why?'

'At Cubs, Akela's doing a Charity Fun Run. We've got to get sponsors for her. She's getting money for a new tent. Maybe two.'

Danny's words give me an idea. Once inside, I get him to show me the form, check with Mum, then email the organiser to ask if I can take part.

Within a couple of hours, an email comes back, with a form for me to download and fill in. I'm just starting to write my name when Mum comes in and orders me up to bed.

'No arguments, Becky,' she says. 'You've got school tomorrow.'

As if I needed reminding, I think, tucking the form into my bag. I check my phone, and there's a text from Sam and one from Charley, telling me her mum wants me to know I'll always be welcome at their place.

The following day, walking into my class is nerve-wracking. Everyone else has already been back a week since half-term. I exchange a brief glance with Leah as someone barges past me. It's Shannon, and the look in her eyes tells me she's out for my blood. I'm shaking, but I try to look calm as I head for my seat at the back of the room.

While Mr MacNamara is calling the register, I take the Fun Run form out of my bag and start to fill it in. Within seconds, Shannon snatches it away from me and is waving it in the air out of my reach.

'Give that back!' I hiss at her as she crumples the form into a ball and chucks it at Masher, hitting him on the back of the neck and causing him to yelp in surprise.

MacNamara looks up. 'What is going on?'

'Nothing, sir,' says Shannon with an angelic smile on her face.

'I'll have that paper, then.'

Masher tosses my form towards Mr MacNamara who catches and uncreases it. He looks it over for a second then holds it out to me.

'This is yours, I take it?'

'Yes, sir.' I take the form from him and I'm about to sit down but I stop. I've got more to say. A lot more.

'I'm taking part in a Fun Run to raise money for the Cardiac Unit where I had my heart operation,' I announce to the class, glancing at Shannon. She's rolling her eyes. 'I know some people don't like the idea of transplants, but, without this new heart inside me, I'd be dead by now. I'm running in memory of my donor and of a friend who needed a new heart, but died before one became available. She was seventeen. Her name was Alice.'

I sit down, and there's an awkward silence before MacNamara gets stuck into calling the last few names on the register, but I don't care what people think any more.

After registration, as everyone's heading off for first lesson, Leah stops by my desk.

'Put me down for a fiver,' she says.

I look up, surprised. 'Sorry?'

'I'll sponsor you.'

'Really?'

She pulls a face. 'Well, if you don't want me to —'

'No please . . . that's great, thanks.'

We smile at each other.

69

As soon as the morning's lessons end, I dive into the girls' changing room, get into my PE kit and head out to the field. I do a few warm-up exercises, then start running. It feels great. At one point, I think I glimpse the bandstand from the park in the distance – I smile and within moments, it fades. My visions no longer freak me, they're just extra memories I've gained over the last few months.

I'm just about to set off round the track when I see someone coming towards me. It's Leah. She's wearing her PE kit too. She's looking at me warily and doesn't say anything for a moment. I bend down and re-tie my trainer lace, uncertain how to react.

'I want to say sorry for telling Jodie about all that stuff you saw,' she says suddenly. 'I didn't realise all the trouble it was going to start.'

Cautiously I glance up at her. She looks back at me anxiously and gives a small sigh. 'I promised you I wouldn't tell anyone. I've been so horrible to you, Becky. I'm really sorry. We . . . Jodie and Alesha and me . . . we all are,' she adds.

I stand up and she hugs me. I don't flinch or try to back away. I hug her back.

'It's OK.'

'And I've so missed being friends.'

'Me too,' I say.

'Mates?' she asks.

I nod. 'Mates.'

We start to jog around the track, at an easy pace. Within minutes, it feels just like old times, when we used to train together. I ask her how the ice-skating went in half-term.

'It was fun, but I spent most of the time on my bum,' she says, pulling a face. 'I was really mean not to ask you.'

'Never mind, you probably saved me a few hundred bruises.'

'Have you heard the latest?' she asks as we start our second circuit, increasing the pace a little.

'Not yet, but you're going to tell me, aren't you?' I say with a grin.

'It's OK, everyone knows. Masher's dumped Shannon. He's found true love, apparently . . .'

We burst into laughter at exactly the same moment.

'Poor Shannon.'

'Oh, she's all right. She was the one who told everyone. She's already asked Wesley out.'

'So who's Masher's lucky girl?' I ask.

'He won't say. But we'll find out at my party on Saturday. You are coming, aren't you?' She smiles, then glances at me and asks, 'Becky . . . that day I saw you on the tube – what was going on?'

I hesitate for a moment. Maybe I will tell her everything that happened one day, but for now I give her the edited version.

'I was getting my life back.' I tell her finally.

70

I look in my bedroom mirror. Everyone is going to be at this party, including Sam – Leah insisted I invite him. Pulling off a blue stripy top, I change into a cream one – an old favourite – but feel annoyed when I see that it too shows my scar.

There's a tap on the door and Gran comes in. 'Ooooh, you look lovely, Becky!' she says, tactfully ignoring the jumble of clothes littering my bedroom floor.

'Thanks, Gran,' I say, noticing a strained look on her face. 'You OK?'

She nods. 'Auntie Vi's convinced the milkman's a Russian spy.' She gives a resigned sigh. 'Now, if Ruby was here, she'd soon talk sense into her.'

'Why don't you go and see her?'

'To America?' She thinks for a second, then shakes her head. 'We're far too old to be gallivanting about . . . unlike you, young lady. Joe asked me to tell you, if you want a lift, you'd better get a move on. He's watching the football with Danny in an hour.'

'Won't be long,' I tell her as she disappears downstairs.

I turn back to the mirror and stare at my reflection. I used to love this cream-coloured top, I think. I'm not vain at all but I know it suits me. I look at my scar, clearly visible above the pretty lace neckline, and suddenly think of Alice. What would she do?

Stuff it, I think. I pick up Leah's present and head downstairs.

'Ready to go!' I call.

71

Joe drops me off outside the Community Hall.

'See you later, Becky,' he says. 'Have a great time.'

'Thanks, Dad.' Shocked, I dart a glance at him. I really, really didn't mean to call him that, it just slipped out. Embarrassed, I quickly scramble out of the car, still managing to catch sight of the grin spreading across his face. And then, for some reason, I catch myself smiling too. As he drives away, he gives me a wave and I wave back.

I walk nervously up the steps to the double doors. Inside, I can hear music blaring – Alesha's boyfriend's band is playing. I can see through the doors that the hall's packed. Leah must have asked half the school. I hesitate for a split second then, realising I'm not petrified of germs any more, step inside.

Leah, Jodie and Alesha are down the far end of the hall. I thread my way through the crowd to where they're standing, in front of the band.

'Becky!' calls Leah.

'Happy birthday!' I say, giving her a hug and handing her my present.

'Thank you!' she says.

'So where's this new boyfriend of yours?' Jodie asks.

I scan the hall. I can't see Sam anywhere. Masher dances up, his elbows flapping wildly. I groan inwardly.

'Becky-Mouse!' he yells over the noise of the music. I try to turn away, but he grabs my hand and starts swinging it.

'Let's dance, babe!'

'No thanks, Masher —'

'But Becky . . .' he yells, just at the very moment the band finishes their song. The room falls silent. '. . . I've always fancied you!' he shouts, completely oblivious to the fact that everyone is now staring at us.

I stare at him, dumbstruck, for a second, then manage to say crossly, 'Well, putting a toad in my lunch bag was a pretty weird way of showing it!'

'No, you're my one true love!' he adds in his usual full-on way.

'That's a shame,' I hear a voice say quietly behind me.

I spin round to see Sam. He's looking at me with his dark, soulful eyes and I feel my heart soar.

'Masher. This is Sam . . .'

'We're together,' Sam adds with a smile, taking my hand and leading me away.

'Wow . . . where's she been hiding him?' I hear Jodie whisper loudly, before Alesha shushes her.

The band starts playing again and Sam holds me in his arms as we dance together. I'm nervous and exhilarated and happy, all rolled into one.

'You look lovely,' he whispers.

'Apart from my scar . . .' I can't help saying.

He pulls me closer to him. 'What scar?' he says gently, then kisses me long and tenderly on the lips.

Waiting

I'm on a playing field filled with three thousand people, waiting for a starting gun to go off. I'm wearing my running vest and shorts, and the top of my scar can be seen but I don't care. It's my battle scar.

Sam's standing next to me, looking a little nervous. Skateboarding's more his thing, but he was determined to take part today.

Leah's doing the run too, and she's on my left, looking cool and relaxed, laughing and chatting to a good-looking lad behind her who's raising money for a charity based in the Caribbean. As we wait, I hear snatches of their conversation and realise, if we don't start soon, they'll have planned a whole trip there together.

Among the crowd of people, loads of them in fancy dress, I spot a group of red-suited Santas – the tallest one scrags down his beard and itches his chin and I realise it's Doctor Sampson with a gang of medics from the hospital. The Santa next to him jumps up and down, waving at me, and I wave back, wondering who it could be. I don't wonder for long, as she pings up her beard and I see it's Natalie.

Up by the railings that edge the field, I spot Mum, Joe and Danny. Gran and Auntie Vi are watching from a safe distance. The pair of them are off to America next week to see their sister Ruby. Gran changed her mind and booked two plane tickets. 'Life's too short,' she told me. 'Got to make the most of it, however old you are.'

'We're seizing the moment,' Auntie Vi added.

The bad news is we've got the cats while they're away.

'Good luck, Becky!' they shout, and Auntie Vi waves a little homemade banner with *Go Rebecca!* written on it in spidery capitals. I'm beyond embarrassment and take it all in my stride.

Masher sits on his bike, watching us. I give him a wave. He may be a complete twazzock and totally unrequited in his (true) love for me, but he went to see Mr Patterson last week and insisted he gave a talk in assembly about Leah and me doing the Fun Run, which got us hundreds more sponsors. Between the three of us, we should raise over a thousand pounds for the Cardiac Unit.

Suddenly, a ripple of excitement works its way through the crowd. The officials are gearing up to start. We're about to go.

Sam turns to me. 'Good luck, Becky,' he says with a smile. My heart beats a little faster, and I realise that I have never been happier.

The starting gun bangs and off we go with three thousand other people. I'm running for Callum, running for Alice . . . running for life.

Desperate Measures

LAURA SUMMERS

Vicky and Rhianna are twins but they couldn't be more different. On their fourteenth birthday, they get a nasty shock.

Their foster parents can't cope and it looks as if Vicky and Rhianna and their younger brother Jamie will have to be split up.

How can they stay together?
Desperate times call for desperate measures . . .

'An exciting adventure with plenty of drama and humour . . . Thought-provoking and moving.'
Books for Keeps

'A fabulous book . . . incredibly poignant.'
Birmingham Post

PENELOPE BUSH

If you could revisit your past, what would you see?

Things are at crisis point for fourteen-year-old Alice. Her mum is ruining her life, her dad's getting remarried, and Sasha, the most popular girl in school, hates her guts . . .

Then a bizarre accident happens, and Alice finds herself re-living her life as a seven-year-old through teenage eyes – and discovering some awkward truths. But can she use her new knowledge to change her own future?

'An amazing book.
Cleverly written, exciting and fast-paced.'
Chicklish

'Ambitious and successful novel that promises well.'
Books for Keeps

Camden Town Tales

The Celeb Next Door

Rosie has lived in Paradise Avenue, Camden Town all her life. As well as the market to hang out at and gigs to go to, there are celebrities to spot, and TV studios where she and her best friends Sky and Vix might get noticed.

When Rosie finds out that the drummer from a chart-topping group is moving into the house next door, she makes it her mission to befriend him. But things don't turn out quite the way she expects . . .

'Camden comes to life in this engaging and fun story of friendship and celebrities.'
Chicklish